Paradise to Perdition
Dani Hatfield

Copyright © 2025 by STEM Publishing

All rights reserved.

No portion of this book may be reproduced in any form without written permission from the publisher or author, except as permitted by U.S. copyright law.

Preface

Hi! Welcome to my first book. Thank you for taking a chance on me by buying my book.

This is book one in my Dark Angel Duet. I will warn you that there is no HEA (that comes in book two).

Without giving too much away, there is implied cheating in this book Read it, you'll find out what I mean by implied, LOL.

I hope you enjoy my writing.

Contents

1. Chapter One — 1
2. Chapter Two — 14
3. Chapter Three — 24
4. Chapter Four — 32
5. Chapter Five — 44
6. Chapter Six — 54
7. Chapter Seven — 62
8. Chapter Eight — 71
9. Chapter Nine — 86
10. Chapter Ten — 97
11. Chapter Eleven — 116
12. Chapter Twelve — 134
13. Chapter Thirteen — 140
14. Chapter Fourteen — 152

Chapter 1

Paradise

Marcus was confused by the message that the lord of Paradise wanted to meet with him. For the most part, the god left him alone to his duties. Apparently, this was an assignment, it would be his first on earth. That was all that he knew so far.

As he made his way to the master's office, he couldn't help but admire the beauty that was Paradise. Of course, that's probably why they had named it that. It was a beautiful place. The water was so clear, you could see the fish swimming below the surface. The flowers were always in bloom and the colors were magnificent. Animals roamed around and they always seemed to be so calm and tranquil. The whole place was serene, as far as that went. Of course, as an angel of Paradise, Marcus really hadn't been anywhere else, he had observed Earth and while it looked fine, it was nothing compared to Paradise.

He was looking forward to this assignment though. He had always wanted to go to earth. It was so different than anything he had ever experienced before. Of course, from his place in Paradise, he could see what earth was like and how it functioned. He found humans fascinating. Physically, they looked pretty much the same as angels, minus the wings of course. They didn't have the same powers that angels had, so he didn't want to be a human. He just found them an interesting subject to study.

He had been able to observe earth for as long as he could remember. It was odd, but it was almost as if he could just will it to happen and he would see a sort of screen or mirror that showed him what was going on down there on Earth.

He made his way up the cobbled path to the top of the highest point in Paradise. The master had a beautiful home there. It was a castle of sorts, not anything that anyone would compare to the typical castle from what Marcus knew. It shimmered in the light that was always present. It wasn't clear, you couldn't see inside from the outside, However, it did look like crystal. It was a beautiful place and so fitting for the lord of Paradise.

So many things fascinated him about Earth though. The first and most basic was that there were males and females. Angles were pretty much just one species or gender, whichever you wanted to call it. Because of the different genders on earth, he had seen both good and bad from both genders. Men often considered themselves superior. Most of the time physically they were, it wasn't always the case. Most men were good hearted and didn't use that added strength to their advantage, but some men did and they treated women poorly. Marcus couldn't abide the idea of anyone, man or woman or angel for that matter taking advantage of others because they had some gene or lack of one that made them think they were superior.

One time, he had observed a situation where a man was irate with a woman and he was very physically aggressive toward her. Maybe it was because he was an angel, he just didn't think anyone should take advantage of someone that was weaker than them.

As an angel, he didn't have to worry about things like relationships and feelings. People on earth seemed to fall in love, and sometimes, that was a wonderful thing. Sometimes it wasn't. If one person loved someone who didn't love them, there was a lot of heartache at times. It seemed so messy. Falling in love, loving someone that didn't love you back. Having someone who loved you that you didn't have any feelings for at all. No, he had seen all of that and it just seemed like too much work. He hoped that whatever it was that the lord of Paradise was sending him to earth for wasn't so quick and hectic that he wouldn't have time to observe the goings on of the day to day lives of humans. He had seen them from afar, it was just that he wanted to know so much more about them. Hopefully he was being sent to comfort some grieving widow or widower or being sent to befriend some small child that had suffered a loss recently in their lives.

He was obviously an empath. He wanted to comfort people, not guide and direct them. No, he believed he would do much better with comforting someone in their time of loss than he would in helping them find the straight and narrow back to a future in Paradise. Not that he wouldn't do that, it just wasn't what he felt he was best at.

Well, standing here hoping and wondering wouldn't do him any good, he might as well go in to the master's office and find out what his assignment was and when he was supposed to start. He made his way to the lord of Paradise so that he could do just that.

"Marcus, please sit down." the master said. When Marcus had set down, the lord continued. "I'm sure Zeriah told you that I have an assignment for you. I need you to go down to earth. I know you have always been fascinated with the planet, and this seemed like the right time to send you."

"Thank you, master." Marcus said. "I'm definitely looking forward to this assignment. So, what is it, grieving widow, orphaned child?"

"Actually, you will be a personal assistant of sorts, and a sort of security job." The lord of Paradise said. "This is the man I need you to befriend and work for." He said turning the screen on his desk. "His name is David Carson. He is going through some things right now that may very well determine which path he goes down in the future. You will have to keep him on the right path even though he is facing some strong enemies that are tempting him to go down a different path. My fear is that if he chooses to remain on the side of morality and justice, they won't like that outcome and may try to harm him."

This sounded like a very difficult situation to Marcus. How was he supposed to keep a man on the straight and narrow? "Uh, what exactly does that mean?" he asked.

"He recently discovered a new product that isn't on the market yet. He needs money." The lord of Paradise gave a shake of his head. "Money can cause many a human to do things that they should never do. Anyway, he needs to find an investor, he doesn't have the money himself. A group of men have offered him the money. They are very unsavory men though and it could bring harm to him or his business if anything goes wrong with them."

"Okay." Marcus said. He wasn't sure he understood fully, however he would do whatever he could.

"David might have other options, if he's willing to consider them. He is trying to find investors, that hasn't gone well so far." The lord continued, "I'm afraid it won't be long until he says yes to some bad men. That can't happen, on the other hand, if he says no, I'm afraid of what these men will do with the rejection of their offer."

"I see." Marcus said. Not exactly what he hoped for, it was still something he was sure he could accomplish. How hard could it be to convince a man to remain on the upright and just path if he was already on it. As far as the protection aspect, it wasn't something he loved doing, although as an angel, he could manage it easily enough. "Well, when do I need to leave?"

"I have a file here that you need to read before you accept the assignment. I want to be sure you understand all of the duties before you agree to go. You won't have the same powers that you have here of course, you need to seem human after all, but you will have the ability to have added physical strength if that is necessary for the tasks you have to accomplish."

"Of course, I'll go and read the file now and be back with any questions as soon as I've finished." Marcus said.

The lord of Paradise turned and there was the lord of Perdition standing in his office. "What do you want?"

"I'm here to let you know, that I will not let this assignment succeed. David is mine, and as far as that goes, I'm sure I can corrupt Marcus too." The dark angel leader said with a snide smile.

"Ha." the lord of Paradise said. "I have full faith in Marcus. He's always been one of my best angels. There is no chance of him turning. And I have full faith that he can and will help David see the benefits of taking the money from his father-in-law. I understand that it's a matter of pride for him, but that pride needs to be gone and he will listen to Marcus."

"I guess we will see when this is finished," the lord of Perdition said.

"Yes, I guess we shall."

As Marcus walked out the door, he was slightly puzzled. He thought he heard voices coming through the door behind him, except there hadn't been anyone else in the room.

What could be so difficult about this assignment that he had to read a file before he went on it? Well, it was his first one on Earth, so maybe there were some guidelines that he had never had to face before. He'd read the file and then accepted the assignment. It wouldn't be a bad thing to go in with extra information that would help him do this more efficiently. There was no way he was going to turn it down. Seeing humans for the first time up close and face to face was just too exciting. This wasn't what he would call his skill set, but he could do it. He was an angel after all, how hard could it be?

He read the file and realized why the lord of Paradise might have been hesitant. It really wasn't a task he would have chosen for himself. It was a man who had been basically a saint until the last few months. He was trying to get his business up and running, he had a young wife that he wanted to provide for, so he was considering taking some money that really shouldn't be used. The people who wanted to 'buy in' to his business lacked a lot of moral character and it was suspected that the money was what people on earth would call 'dirty'. It most likely came from businesses that weren't moral or legal and they were trying to do something that was called laundering it through a legitimate business. The man, David Carson had been trying to find money through the proper channels, but no one seemed to want to loan him money or buy into his plan, except the wrong element. It was also possible that this 'triad', as they were referred to, were putting pressure on other possible investors to keep them from saying yes.

If Marcus did accept the assignment, it would be his duty to try his best to steer David away from the current potential investors toward keeping his business clean. Unfortunately, the people who wanted to invest weren't likely to take no for an answer and they might in turn try to harm Mr. Carson.

The file also detailed what his situation would be. For the most part, he would be perceived as human by anyone he met. He wouldn't have any angel characteristics other than some extraordinary physical strength if he did need to defend his charge against the men who may want to harm him. He wouldn't be able to reveal himself as an angel to anyone. And his powers would only be available to him if he or his charge were under a threat.

There were also details about the man himself and his young wife, it included pictures of both and a basic biography. They had been married just a little over a year. In Marcus' opinion, that was probably at least a part of why the man was considering an investment that was less than favorable if it would help him get a better nest egg for he and his wife. Especially if they were considering having children at some point in the not-too-distant future.

If banks were turning him down, and he was feeling the pressure to make sure that his wife was provided for both now and in the future, he might take risks that he normally wouldn't even consider. Either way, it sounded like he had always been an above board businessman and it likely wouldn't take much effort to show him that this path was not the one he should go down. Marcus was going to accept the assignment. He really wanted to go to Earth, and this assignment didn't sound like anything he couldn't handle. He went back to the lord of Paradise and told him he was ready for the assignment to begin.

As Marcus walked away, he had a sense that the master hadn't been completely convinced that he was the right person for this job, but he did agree to send Marcus, so maybe it was just his imagination that he didn't seem completely in favor of his own decision.

While the lord of Paradise had no doubt that Marcus could handle the actual assignment, he did have a thought somewhere in the back of his mind exactly how Marcus would handle being primarily human. It was his first assignment, and he had always had a fascination of sorts with humans and Earth.

He had to trust that Marcus would do the assignment well and that he would come out of it the same angel he had always been.

Perdition

The lord of Perdition looked at the angel sitting on the other side of his desk. "Esmerelda this is one of the most important assignments I have ever given you. You absolutely must, without question, get Marcus to fall from grace with the lord of Paradise. Seduce him, make him fall in love with you. What ever it takes. I have to win this battle."

"I understand." she said. "So, you have the real Desire secured somewhere and I'm going to take her place. Even her husband won't be able to tell the difference when we are together. Is there a preference as to how I handle things with David?"

"Not really." the master said. "I don't really care if he lives or dies, although him dying makes even more of a failure out of Marcus. So, maybe I do care in that sense. If you can help push him toward taking the money from the father-in-law rather than the triad, it would definitely put him in danger of angering them and causing retribution."

"I think that's going to be the easier part too, from what I read in the file. Desi would totally push him to take the money from her father. She is a daddy's girl after all. The sun rises and sets with that man in her mind. If she had any indication that her husband had the potential to expand his business, she would go to her father with or without his permission." she said.

"I have confidence in you. I'm sure you will do well with this assignment." he said. "As far as your usual powers, you will have access to them as needed."

Esmeralda stood up and she felt the weight of her wings fall away she was transformed into a human and within seconds, she was sitting behind a desk in an office watching Marcus come through the door.

Chapter 2

It seemed like only a snap of the fingers and Marcus was on earth in some sort of a small office building. He assumed this was the head of Carson enterprises, the business his assignment owned. Apparently, the man had hired a personal assistant/financial advisor and the man he thought he had hired was actually Marcus. Fortunately, the information to do both parts of the job had divinely been imparted to him when he landed on earth because otherwise, he would not be able to make a good impression on his new employer.

"Excuse me, Miss." Marcus said to the woman sitting at the reception desk, "I believe I have an appointment with David Carson."

The woman looked up from the tablet she had been working with and Marcus had a sharp intake of breath. She was the most beautiful creature he had ever seen. His brain told him that he should have referred to her as the most attractive woman he had ever seen, although that wasn't much of a stretch, he hadn't seen any women before other than his long-distance observations from Paradise. So, he grouped her with every other creature he had ever seen, angels, beasts, sea creatures or anything else he had ever experienced.

She had long brownish blonde hair and a beautiful smile. Her eyes were a magnificent blue, a color that sometimes graced the skies in Paradise. Her skin was lightly bronzed, although not overly so. It was probably mostly attributed to the fact that they didn't have different genders in Paradise, but he was fascinated with this woman. She had a shape that wasn't like anything that he had ever seen. She had curves and well, he wasn't really sure what they were called.

He definitely needed to do more reading and studying of the human race.

"Good morning, you must be Marcus Johnson." the beautiful woman said. "I'll let my husband know that you are here."

Well, that told him all he needed to know. She was David's wife and therefore, no matter how attractive she was, she was not someone he should spend any time with other than to work with her. That was going to be difficult, because he really did want to see her more than just sitting at a desk when he walked into work every day. However, that wasn't going to happen.

It sounded odd to him to have the Johnson part added on, but he had been told that all humans had a last name, so he had been assigned one of the more common ones. Part of the file that he had been given and had gone through more than a few times had included all of the correspondence between 'him' and David. It hadn't been him of course, this had all been done by someone that the lord of Paradise had assigned to do the preparations. He knew exactly what 'he' had said and who 'he' was supposed to be. He knew what background and qualifications 'he' had that had landed the job. He wasn't sure if there had actually been a man named Marcus Johnson that he had suddenly replaced, but he was sure that the emails had been done by someone else in Paradise.

He heard the woman talking to a voice that seemed to be coming out of some box on her desk. He was pretty sure it was what was called an intercom. He had read the debrief after he had accepted the assignment about what things were called here on earth so that he would fit in and not be out of place. He had been imparted with the knowledge of how to use a phone and a computer. It seemed like the intercom either was easy to learn or was something he wouldn't need to know because it hadn't been completely explained to him like most things had.

The lord of Paradise hadn't been wrong when he said that for the most part, Marcus didn't have any of his angel powers or knowledge. Usually on an assignment, the angel was imparted with the ability to just comprehend the place he had been sent. He wasn't sure why the Master had chosen to not give it to him telepathically, he was sure he could learn and he was fast on his feet and could manage to cover for the things that he didn't know by studying more while he was here. Being an empath, he could often pick up on things by reading their feelings which helped him have an idea of the thoughts of those surrounding him. He sat in one of the seats that seemed to take two sides of the room to wait for David to come out or the woman to give him further instruction.

A few minutes later, a man came from someplace down what appeared to be a short hallway. Marcus stood to greet who he assumed to be his temporary boss. He held out his hand and asked, "David Carson, I assume."

"Yes, Marcus, I'm happy to finally meet you." David said, shaking the angel's hand. "I'm sorry that our correspondence so far has been by email, but things have been hectic around here. Hence my need to hire someone like you."

"Oh, that's fine." Marcus said. "I'm just happy for the assignment."

David looked at him rather curiously at the word assignment, so he made a mental note to change it to position in the future.

"Great, come on back and I'll show you your office space and then we can sit down and talk about how things are going to proceed going forward." David turned to the woman at the desk and said, "Desi, hold my calls unless it's important. I'll let you know when our meeting is done."

Oh, this assignment wasn't going to be bad at all, Desi thought to herself. The man she was supposed to try to seduce was an absolute god. Well, not in the traditional sense, but he did look a lot like the statues of Greek gods that she had seen in the books she had read about the history of earth. She had been given a very human body, and it was already reacting to the virility of that man, or angel, whichever you wanted to consider him at this point. The lord of Perdition must really like her to give her an assignment that was going to be so much fun. Of course, she had always been successful in everything he had ever asked her to do, so it was probably not hard to understand why he had chosen her for this assignment.

As for the body she had been put it, it was pretty enough. Nothing glamorous, but she was a beautiful woman. She could live with what she had been given and make this work.

They walked down the short hallway, and David showed him a door almost at the end of the hallway. "That's your office there. I'll let you get a chance to set it up to your preferences after we talk about what's going on and what I'm needing your help with." They continued down to the end of the hall. "This is my office. I usually leave the door open unless I'm on an important phone call. Even then, give a short knock and I'll most likely let you in. You are my assistant after all. Let's have a seat and I'll update you on where things are."

David sat behind his desk, and Marcus sat in one of the two chairs in front of it. "Just let me know where you need me to jump in, boss." Marcus said.

"Well, as I've been telling you in the emails, I'm trying to expand my business. It's doing okay right now. Kind of a 'holding its own' type of situation. However I want more. I'm hoping you can come alongside me and suggest other options. We can brainstorm about ways to make that happen, if you have any input, I'm open to hearing it. I've looked at the traditional route, local banks and all that. I haven't been in business long enough or I haven't demonstrated the amount of profit margin that they want me to have to be able to approve a traditional business loan."

Marcus nodded. "I understand, so now you're looking for ways to either change their minds or get the financing from another source."

"Exactly." David agreed. "I need to keep it legal, at least as legal as possible. The woman you met out in the outer office is my wife. She's the reason I want to expand. We've been talking about having children and I need to make sure she and any possible future children are provided for for the long term. I'm healthy and all that, but we never know when we could be walking across the street and get hit by a car. Am I right?"

Marcus had no idea if he was right or not. He would agree with him because it seemed the most prudent thing to do. "Right, yeah, I get what you are saying. We never know what tomorrow might bring." Did that sound too 'angel like'?

Apparently, that was what he was expected to say because David just nodded. "Anyway, I don't want to go down any path that would leave me vulnerable, I need to figure out how to have this all set up for the future. So, any guidance or input that you can offer will be highly appreciated."

"Of course." Marcus agreed. "I'll look through the files of what you've done already and take some time to evaluate possible future moves. Hopefully, I'll have some suggestions in the next few days."

"That would be great." David said. "I'm not trying to put a time crunch on this, I just don't want to leave it alone for too long, if you know what I mean."

"I do." Marcus said. He wasn't really sure that he understood every single word the man had said, but he at least understood the principle.

"Great. I'll let you go get settled in your office. I'm going to take my beautiful wife out for lunch." David said.

Marcus made his way back down the hall several feet to the door that David had pointed out as his. He actually was going to go through the files to see what the man had attempted already and try to find out who these other potential investors were. He knew that he was supposed to steer David away from them, so the more he knew about them the better. Fortunately, the lord of Paradise had imparted him with the knowledge to use modern earth technology like computers and phones. There was something called Google that he had been told could be a valuable source of information. Just before he closed his office door, he watched David and Desire walk to the main office door and turn the lock before they closed it behind them. Just before they had disappeared through the door, the woman had turned and gave him a very warm smile. He was sure she was just being kind to try to welcome him to the company. At least, he assumed that was what the smile was.

Chapter 3

Marcus started with the top file folder and began to work his way down the stack. It appeared that the money for the start-up of the business had come from the wedding present Desire's father had given them. If he had that kind of money, maybe he would be willing to help them expand their nest egg. That would be the first suggestion he gave to David. On the other hand, the man may have been saving for years to be able to give his daughter a hundred thousand dollars for a wedding gift. He may not have a stash of money that he could invest. Still it was a better option than laundering money for the mob. Actually, Marcus wasn't sure they were actually from a mob, however, the things he read made it seem like they were definitely unsavory characters.

He kept digging. As David had said, he had approached every bank and credit union within a one-hundred-mile radius and had been turned down by them all. He had searched online for other companies outside of his own local area and again, the results had been dismal. Most cited a lack of credit history and the length of time the business had been operating as the reason for their denial. If the father-in-law wasn't an option maybe it would be better to just put things on hold for a year or so and try again. He could tell that David was anxious to make it happen now, but was the risk worth it just to speed things along?

Marcus also opened up the computer, thankful it didn't have a password and tried a Google search for any information beyond what he already knew about the company and its owner. He was going to check into the wife too, to see if he could find out anything about her father or her family. A voice in the back of his brain said that wasn't his only motive. He told the voice to be quiet. Yes, she was a beautiful woman, he wouldn't deny that. She was also the wife of his assignment, and he was sure that lusting after her wasn't a good idea. That didn't mean that he couldn't admire her from afar. That wasn't really something he could keep from doing anyway. If a being finds beauty in the world, he couldn't help but enjoy it and savor it, could he?

A part of him was surprised at the reaction of his own heart, mind and body. An angel didn't really have those things. The physical make up was just different than that of a human. Except the lord of Paradise had told him that he was going to be primarily human other than a few of the abilities he may need to perform his task. It was going to take some time to get used to experiencing things like this. He knew that he would have added strength, if he needed it to guard David. He could quickly learn things that he read or was exposed to. He himself couldn't die or get sick, but other than that he was mostly physically human.

He forced himself to get back into the files to dig out more information. David wasn't from a wealthy family, they were upper middle class from what he could tell. He was fortunate that the lord had imparted him with the basic human knowledge, otherwise he wouldn't have had a clue what the difference was.

Desi's family, on the other hand, was quite wealthy. Her father seemed to be a well known businessman with a lot of businesses that he either owned or at least owned a large portion of. He would definitely be a good possible source for the investment. But there had to be some reason that David hadn't gone to him.

There really wasn't much more information that was of any help for the assignment. There was no mention at all who the men were that potentially wanted to invest. That didn't surprise Marcus. Putting names and information like that into the file would have run the risk that Desi or her father might find out who they were and it was unlikely that they would be in favor of the investment.

Part of the knowledge he had been given was the names of the men who were trying to convince David to take money from them. He was going to spend some time trying to get as much knowledge about them as he possibly could.

David and Desi returned from lunch, and David poked his head into Marcus' office. "Have you had a chance to get up to speed, or do you need more time?"

"No, I think I have the basics anyway." Marcus said. "I'll keep them handy in case any other questions arise."

"Great, come into my office and we'll see if we can form a plan." David said before he walked down the hall. When Marcus sat across from him, David said, "Any insight, any thoughts?"

"Well, my first thought would be your father-in-law." Marcus said.

"Not possible." David said immediately. "Any other thoughts?"

"Wait, there has to be more than just 'not possible'" Marcus was puzzled. "Does he not have the money? He seems pretty wealthy. Did you already ask, and he told you no? Give me more to go on."

David paused for a moment closed his eyes and pinched the bridge of his nose. Of course there was a reason for that. He wanted to be a self-made man, not a man who was only a success because his father-in-law was rich. His older brother had always been the one to go farther and faster than David. It was already too late to become a wealthy businessman before his brother did, but he would do it without the help of his wife's family. His brother had reached out to investors and they had seemed all too happy to give him money for his start up. Within three years, he was using the capital from his business to invest in other businesses. He had become a millionaire, hell, maybe even a billionaire for all David knew. He and his brother had never been close, and his brother had always been better than him at anything they had ever attempted.

After a moment, he finally said, "Yes, he definitely has the money. No, I haven't asked him. There's a reason for that though. He really didn't want Desi to marry me. I'm not from the 'right stock'. I honestly believe that the only reason he gave us the money as a wedding present was that it was the same amount he had given his other children and far be it from Kenneth Davis to let anyone think that he was playing favorites amongst his children. I also think part of it was a fear that people might think he was financially struggling if he didn't give her the same gift. If he had his choice, he would have given it to her and not to me, however, my wife has always believed in this business and my dream, so she wanted us to use it this way. He would make a mockery out of me if I asked for more. It would also give him ammunition to try to convince Desi that I really was a loser after all."

"Ah, well it would be the perfect solution if it weren't for all of that." Marcus said. "The other option is to just wait six to twelve months and try again. I know you're anxious to expand, but you would look more favorable to banks if the business is solid for a longer time period."

David gave a deep sigh and said, "I know. I do, I know that, I just don't feel like I have a year to wait for this. There are other companies that open every day doing basically the same thing as we do here. If one of them gets a jump on some of the technology, we lose the market altogether. I can't afford that; we have to be cutting edge."

What else could Marcus say? He wasn't supposed to know about the offer the group of men had made to David. It wasn't mentioned in the files. He couldn't just drop it into the conversation. "I understand, but I'd be cautious about taking money from anyone that wasn't fully open and honest." Hopefully, that sounded like good wisdom he would give to anyone who didn't want him to know that he was considering a loan from less than savory people.

"I know, I know." David said. "It's just so damned frustrating to be in this position."

"I understand, today is my first day here. Give me a chance to look things over and see if I can find a better way of doing things." Marcus encouraged.

"Okay, for now." David said. "Thanks for taking this all so seriously though. I really appreciate it. Let me know if you come up with any other brainstorms."

Marcus stood up and started to walk out of the office when David called him back.

"Desi wanted me to ask you to come to dinner this Friday. It will give you a chance to settle into your new apartment before going out to socialize."

"I'd like that." Marcus said. "I'll be sure to thank her for the invitation." He walked out of David's office and started down the hall toward his own office.

He debated with himself to possibly go out to thank Desi now. It would give him the chance to see her beauty again, but he opted for professionalism and went back to his office to focus on work.

Chapter 4

Marcus's first week was pretty much just a 'learning what the company was all about' type of thing and getting to know David and Desi more, at least on a professional level. He could understand David's desire to expand. The security industry was growing fast. The first company to come up with the technology to take it to the next level was going to be touted throughout the world as the best in the business. They would pretty much be able to go anywhere they wanted to with their company. The problem was, it took a lot of research to get there, and then a whole lot more development to put the products out there. That was going to take a large amount of money just to hire the researchers. There was no telling how quickly they would have anything ready for development and distribution and if you ended up not being the first, you pretty much just threw your money away in the research.

He wished that the lord of Paradise had just given him the perfect solution to the money issues, but he hadn't. That was part of the assignment. To keep David on the straight and narrow and discourage him from going down the less than perfect path. The problem with that situation though was that it was also possible that keeping him from taking their money would also make them want to harm or even murder him. Which was also part of the assignment, to keep the man alive and away from harm. If they had ultimately decided that his business had something that they wanted to have control of, they wouldn't just let him say no without any pressure to change his mind.

On Friday, he made his way to David's home for dinner. He was so thankful that the lord of Paradise had at least imparted him with the basic understanding of modern technology on earth. He had a cell phone, and it had something called GPS on it. He also miraculously knew how to drive a car. All things that were very welcome to someone who hadn't spent five minutes on earth before the past Monday.

He pulled up to a nice, although not large home. It was in a neighborhood that seemed to be family friendly if the bikes and toys in front yards were any indication. He wasn't sure if he should park on the street or the driveway, he saw several other cars on the street, so he felt it was safe to do the same.

As he walked up to the front door of the house, David opened it and greeted him with a handshake. "Marcus, welcome to our home. Come on in. Can I get you anything to drink? Wine, coffee, water?"

"Water will be fine, thank you." He stepped into the house and found a warm and welcoming atmosphere. Again, it wasn't anything that showed wealth, but it was comfortable. He assumed that Desi had put her entire wedding gift into the business rather than needing a large home.

There was a comfortable couch and chair set, tables and stands that had little figurines and pictures on them. The pictures on the wall were primarily of people that Marcus assumed to be family members or friends and there were several pictures that were from their wedding. There wasn't any art per se. At least not anything that one would recognize and something famous or even a replica of something famous. It was more about their lives and the people that were important parts of it.

David came back out with a glass of water with ice and a lemon slice and a lime slice. "Thank you." Marcus said.

"You're welcome, although the fruit and ice are all Desi. I'm a man, water is water, she's always been a gracious hostess and wants the guest to have the best." David said handing the glass to Marcus. "She says dinner will be ready in about ten minutes."

"That's fine." Marcus said. That was one thing that he hadn't been sure how his master would set things up. Would he need to eat, just as humans did? Would he be able to eat, but not need it to survive? Fortunately, that was one of the things that had been left up to him, he didn't need to eat, however he could eat if food were available. So that people didn't wonder if there was something odd about him.

They sat on a couch and quietly, David said, "Don't mention the financial stuff from the office to Desi okay? I'm not telling her about the issues finding an investor. She knows that I hope to expand someday, but I'm afraid if she knows my struggle, she'll go to her father. I'm sure he would give her the money, however, as I told you before, I don't want to be beholden to him. He would lord it over my head for years to come."

Marcus just nodded in agreement. He wouldn't make promises to anything of the sort. No, he wasn't going to go running to Desi first thing. He also wouldn't promise to never mention it to her if that ended up being what he needed to do to keep David alive and out of prison. He would do his best to honor the man's request if at all possible.

It was odd though that David seemed so sure that the man would hold it against him when there had been no indication that the man had ever done anything of the kind. Desi obviously loved her father so her opinion would be biased, but David seemed more opposed to it than the average person would be. However, he couldn't find out why David was so sure about it without asking Desi, and for now, he had agreed not to do that.

They talked about normal everyday things, well, not really every day for Marcus, he did his best to keep up with the chit chat. He did a lot of nodding and saying things like 'definitely' and 'oh for sure'. Luckily, David tended to enjoy talking so there weren't really any lulls in the conversation.

Desi peaked her head around the corner David had disappeared behind earlier and announced that the food was ready. When they sat at the table, she apologized that the meal wasn't anything fancy.

Marcus wasn't really the one to judge what human foods were, or what was good or not, but his taste buds really seemed to light up when he tasted the dinner Desi had prepared. Was that a thing? They technically couldn't lite up, could they spark? Well, whatever the terminology was, they were very happy with what they were tasting.

"Don't mind my Desi." David began. "She was raised with servants and cooks and if it isn't filet mignon or escargot, it's slumming. I keep telling her that I've always loved the more simple meals like what I was raised with. And I'm very appreciative of her cooking skills. I can't afford to hire a cook and if I had to do the cooking, we'd be eating burgers, eggs or sandwiches for every meal."

"Oh, my parents aren't quite that bad." Desi began. "Yes, I grew up in a house of privilege as they say, but I'm just a simple girl who wants to be happy with the man I love. I would eat whatever you prepared if I wasn't able to cook and you had to take on the task." She seemed completely devoted to her marriage and that she was supportive of her husband. Maybe the touches when she had brought him coffee the other day hadn't been what Marcus had thought they were. Her hand had brushed his, and she had put a hand on his shoulder at one point while they were talking. Or maybe she was just the type of person that was a physical contact sort. Since he technically didn't have to sleep, it left him with lots of time to watch movies and explore the internet to try to understand humans and their relationships better.

She turned to Marcus and said, "On the other hand, fire up the grill in the backyard, and David can come up with some amazing things. They are still simple, although, the spices and seasonings make them out of this world."

David wasn't really blushing, however he didn't seem comfortable with the praise either. "Oh, Desi, you may be just a little biased on that feeling. I cooked for your parents that one time and all they did was complain that it was too dry and too overcooked."

Ah, so that explained some more things about why David wouldn't go to his father-in-law about the money. They hadn't treated him well and didn't seem to like anything about him.

"This is delightful, Desi." Marcus said. He hoped he could at least cut some of the tension that he was feeling at the dinner table. Obviously, Desi loved her family, imperfect as they may be, then again, he had learned that it was a status known as 'being human'.

He had started out calling her by her full name, she had told him that if they were going to be friends, she insisted that he call her Desi. He had not wanted to seem too forward, but he was happy that she considered him a friend. He needed to keep his mind on his assignment though, and the fact that she was a married woman. Wishing there was a way that he could have her to himself was utterly ridiculous. He was an angel; she was a human. It wasn't even feasible that they could actually have a relationship, even if she wasn't married to his assignment, it wasn't something that could happen. He would be called back to Paradise at some point and she would go on with her human life here on earth.

The conversation included a lot of questions for Marcus about where he was from and what he had done before he moved here. Of course, the lord of Paradise had given him a plausible back story to share with anyone who asked. He had lived in Dallas before coming here. He was a personal assistant to the CEO of a large financial institution. That had actually been one of the selling points that had made David hire him for this position. He had a background in finances. Well, he at least had knowledge about the financial industry imparted to his brain before being sent down to earth so it seemed like he knew what he was doing with it all. One of the great things about being an angel, apparently, you could learn everything that took a human years to obtain in a matter of minutes if it was imparted to you by your master.

He did take the opportunity to ask Desi about her family. He got a couple of odd looks from David because he seemed to be going down a path that he was told not to go down. He would assure the man that it was just casual conversation that anyone would expect a new friend to be curious about. He asked David similar questions. He needed to know as much about them as he could find out. He had to understand why David was so against Desi speaking to her father. He understood that it was a pride thing to a point, but it seemed like there was more. Like he couldn't face the man thinking he might need help in any situation.

David didn't seem overly fond of his older brother. Although he didn't say anything specific, he talked about the man with a bit of a sneer on his face and his eyes darkened over a bit.

After they were done eating, Desi began to clear the dishes. Marcus offered to help her with that.

"Oh, you don't need to." she stated.

"No, you provided such a delicious meal, it's the least I can do." Marcus debated.

"If you insist."

He started piling the dirty plates and flatware into a stack and carried them into the kitchen. Desi followed with her own stack of things. "So, what are you going to do on your first full weekend in our city?" she asked him.

"Mostly, I'm just going to try to learn my way around. Figure out where things are. I don't know where many things are. Fortunately, I did find a grocery store, so I haven't been going hungry, but that's about it." Not that he would actually go hungry, since he didn't need to eat, except he had found that he liked the taste of some foods so he bought things when he wanted to explore. So far, mushrooms were not to his liking, and he had discovered that there were so many varieties of cheese that he could try a different one every day for a long time before he ran out of options. So far, he hadn't found one that he didn't like.

"I'd be happy to show you around a little if you'd like me to." Desi offered.

"Oh, I couldn't take you away from David on a weekend. I am sure you have plans already." Marcus said.

"Actually, no, I don't have anything planned and David won't mind. Between living together and working together, sometimes it's nice to do something separate on the weekend." She assured.

"Well, if you're sure, that would be great. I'd appreciate it very much."

"Just jot down your address and I'll swing by and pick you up. It's easier if I drive since I know my way around rather than trying to tell you where to turn and all that." She handed him a pencil and a small note pad that had been on the countertop.

He wrote his address down and they went into the living room where David was sitting smoking a cigar. He offered one to Marcus, he turned it down. Marcus was pretty sure that he heard Desi say something about it being a nasty habit. He wasn't positive that she had said it, because it had been barely audible, but angels did have really good hearing.

Desi had to plan to begin to make a move to get Marcus interested in her. She was glad that he had agreed to spend the day with her. She would do her best to be kind, although, she planned to also be very flirty. She would touch him in small ways that wouldn't seem completely inappropriate. Just a hand on his arm or a touch of his hand. Maybe running her foot up and down his leg under the table.

She would begin her seduction in such a simple manner that it wouldn't feel like seduction at all.

Chapter 5

The following morning, Marcus was outside of his apartment building waiting for Desi to pull up. She turned onto his street in her little gray Mercedes, undoubtedly a gift from her father. It didn't look like it was one of the newest models, but it was a Benz just the same. She pulled up to the curve right in front of him and he got into the car. "Nice wheels." he said. Knowing the modern lingo definitely came in handy.

"Thanks, it was an engagement present from my daddy." She had a beaming smile. It was obvious that she adored her father, and he likely felt the same way. The sticking point in their relationship had been when she had married someone he considered beneath her station in life.

"How long have you and David been married?" he asked. He already knew this, it was in the file he had been given, he just thought it seemed like the type of thing that a new friend would ask.

"Just about two years." Desi said. "My daddy tried to talk me out of marrying David for a long time, but I just had my mind made up. I wasn't going to budge."

"Well, when you're in love, I suppose it's pointless to try to delay it." Marcus said.

Desi hesitated for a brief second and then said, "Yes, I guess so."

What was that pause, was it possible that there was a rift in their relationship, or maybe she was no longer as sure as she had thought she was. Briefly, Marcus wondered if a part of her wanting to marry David had been just to piss her father off. Some spoiled debutants enjoyed creating waves just for the sake of creating waves.

They drove for a while with Desi pointing out places he might have an interest in going in the future. Mostly it consisted of the library and a few galleries and museums. When it was almost one in the afternoon, she suggested that they stop for lunch. Marcus agreed, and they ended up at what Marcus assumed was one of the more expensive restaurants in town. It looked very lavish to him anyway. So, Desi was still keeping up with her expensive tastes, despite David being a struggling new business owner. Most likely, her 'daddy' as she referred to him, was sending her some money on the side.

When she parked, she didn't get out of the car at first. Marcus realized that she was probably waiting for him to be a gentleman and open the door for her. So, he went around and held her door. She got out and wrapped her hand around his bicep.

Marcus couldn't mistake the touch of the side of her breast against his arm. It wasn't just a light brush; she was pressing herself up against him. He knew that he was supposed to be an angel, but apparently, there was enough human in him that he enjoyed that contact with her. He placed his hand over hers to add to the contact with her. He had been watching movies and he had seen men do that in some of them. He realized that you couldn't always believe everything that you saw in a movie, however simple things like being a gentleman were easy to follow and mimic.

They were seated at a table that overlooked a beautiful park. No doubt one of the benefits of being well known here. Several people had greeted Desi as they had walked behind the Matre'd.

"This seems like a really nice place, do you and David come here often?" Marcus asked.

"No, this isn't really David's type of place, I meet one or both of my parents here sometimes." she explained. "I have been coming here with them since this place opened when I was a teenager. I guess I've just always liked it."

When Marcus looked at the menu, he could tell this definitely wasn't David's type of place. His boss seemed more like a burger and fries type of guy with an occasional steak. This list included extravagant dishes and things that took a small paragraph to describe. He couldn't mistake the feeling of Desi's toes sliding up the side of his ankle. He wasn't ignorant enough to not believe that she was intentionally flirting with him. The problem was, he didn't know why. Was she unhappy in her marriage, did she just like to be flirtatious? He just didn't have enough knowledge of how things went to be sure of the reason for her actions. He wouldn't call her out on it, he didn't want to embarrass her, he did try to shift a little further away. He was new to all of this, if he was interpreting things correctly, Desi was a big flirt. At least she seemed to be flirting with him, then again, he was an angel, and he might be reading it completely wrong.

The food was delicious, and Marcus enjoyed it very much. When the bill came, Marcus insisted on paying. After all, she was doing him a big favor by driving him all around the area showing him things that he might want or need to know the location of someday.

When they got back out to her car, Marcus opened the door for her and while he was holding it for her, she leaned in and gave him a kiss on the cheek. "Thank you for lunch Marcus."

He was not going to read too much into this stuff. At least, he was trying to. He kept telling himself that she wasn't trying to start anything with him, she was just obviously a very friendly type of person and expressed her emotions with physical gestures.

They spent another two hours with her showing him where the movie theater and malls were. By the time they were done, Marcus felt like he had a much better handle on how to find the things he may want or need to access in the future.

Desi hadn't missed Marcus moving away from her at the table, she didn't let it last for long, she moved towards him again a few minutes later. Oh, she made it seem like she was just getting more comfortable on the bench, but she still ended up closer to him than she had been before she had run her toes up his leg. If he kept moving, he would end up pinned in a corner with nowhere to go. Desi didn't really have a problem with that idea.

On Monday, Marcus walked into the office and found Desi sitting at her desk as she usually was. She gave him a warm smile and a wink. She had never done that before.

"David would like to have a meeting with you at ten to go over whatever you have been working on."

"Got it, thanks." he smiled back. She was a very kind and beautiful woman, he wasn't going to be cold or rude to her. If it weren't for the fact that she was married to his boss, he would try to date her. He had found a channel on the TV called the Hallmark channel and there were all sorts of movies about people falling in love. He thought it looked like a really happy thing to be, in love. It sounded so amazing.

He took off his jacket and pulled out the files he had gone through them several times before. He was hoping that something new would jump out at him. He wasn't sure what it could possibly be, he had gone through these files so many times already. Then, he saw something that he had never seen before. In fact, he was sure that it hadn't ever been there before. In the margin of one of the pages, clearly in David's handwriting was the word 'Dynacorp'. It had been crossed off, but it was clearly there and was still legible. Finally, he had an opening to slip in some thoughts about the investment company and his fear that they weren't completely on the up and up.

When it was ten, he made his way down the hall to David's open door. He still gave a short knock on the door frame, just to be sure that the man was ready for him.

"Marcus, come on in." David said gesturing to the chair across from him. "So, you've had a chance to go through the files on what I've done so far. Did it give you any ideas on where I can get the money I need?"

"Well, I don't know why I hadn't noticed this before, but this morning, I spotted this in the margin on one of the papers." He pulled out the specific one and pointed to the word he had spotted. "It made me curious, since it was a lead I hadn't followed up on before. I did some checking into Dynacorp and I have to say that I'm not sure they are a good idea. There isn't anything that is obvious or provable, they just seem rather shady to me."

David looked at the paper as if he had no idea where that word had come from. "Yeah, I'm not really sure why I jotted that down there. I've not really given them much consideration as a perspective lender. Although, I don't know if there is anyone else that would give me the money. Any other thoughts?"

"Well, not a lot of them. I know that you don't want to hear this, honestly, your best option is still Desi's father."

"And as I've said before, that's not an option I am willing to consider." David said adamantly.

"I understand that he wasn't in favor of your marriage, and I get that it's a matter of pride for you, but if the choices are taking money from him or not getting it at all, you have to decide which is more important. Just make it a loan. You don't need to sign a partnership agreement with him or anything. If the projections are even partially accurate, once the product takes off, you will be able to pay him back and be well on your way to your own financial empire."

"It's not that simple."

"I know." Marcus agreed. "I definitely don't feel comfortable with the thought of taking money from the Dynacorp group. I just get an odd vibe about them. It's like they aren't completely above board on things. It makes me wonder if they have ties to the mob or to some illegal activity. I haven't found any proof of that yet, it's just a gut instinct I guess."

"I know, I've heard rumors, but none of them has ever been proven." David said. "I can't afford to turn down a viable offer if they aren't into anything illegal. I need to get ahead of the competition."

"I understand that. Although there aren't even rumors out there that anyone else is considering anything like this technology. While I understand that you can't wait forever, I don't think that taking this a little slow for now is a bad idea until we know for sure who those men are and even consider other investment groups. I'll do the research on anything I can find and forward it on to you so you can make first contact."

"Okay, I'll wait, but not for long." David said. "I haven't heard any rumors about anyone else even considering this either, and I already have the ground level research done so I am one step ahead in that way. Although I don't think I can wait more than a few weeks, maybe a month." He put his head down and focused on the paperwork he had on his desk that he had been going through before Marcus had knocked on the door. It was clear that the conversation was done for now.

Chapter 6

Over the next few days, Marcus tried to look into every possible investment company he could find. None seemed to be in a position to invest in something that might take a while before the payouts came back to them. With the technology that David wanted to develop, it was going to take time to complete research and development and then the testing would begin. It would be likely to be up to two years before they were ready to take the product to market. He could get preliminary patents before starting full production so that his property was secure, but profits were what mattered to investors and in today's society where things advanced so fast, some might be hesitant to invest because there was always the chance that bigger and better would come out before David had his day in the spotlight.

Inventing a product was much safer than inventing technology. At least as far as the timelines went. If your product was built, testing went fairly quickly. It either worked, or it didn't. Technology was a completely different story. Just because it seemed to work on the surface, there were always bugs that showed up when least expected. Consumers understood that there would be a bug here or there, but only to a point before they didn't want to keep trying.

Marcus was very aware of the fact that Desi stopped into his office at least once a day to 'chat'. He was also very aware that she always unbuttoned at least one button more than she usually had when she did come down the hall heading anywhere except his office. He knew that he shouldn't even look at her, he just didn't seem to be able to help himself. A human woman's body definitely held a certain amount of appeal, at least for him. He would never act on his attraction, what could it hurt to look and enjoy?

Early Friday afternoon, David announced that he was going out for the rest of the day. He didn't say where he was going, but Marcus was pretty sure he had a good idea. He was going to talk to someone about getting money. Whether or not it was the triad, Marcus wasn't sure, it would be likely that he was at least keeping them on the hook just in case nothing else worked out. Marcus firmly believed that the man really didn't want to take money from them, but if nothing else would work out, he would do it. He wanted so badly to make a name for himself.

Marcus was certain that that fact was partly based on his recent marriage and who his Father-in-law was. He wanted to prove to both of them that he could do this without the family money. The problem was that Marcus wasn't sure that he could. Sometimes, you had to decide between your pride and your hopes. It would give David a chance at success either way. His product, if it could get out there quickly, really was revolutionary and would likely make him a lot of money, but he may have to realize that his two choices were his father-in-law or the triad and of the two, the father-in-law was definitely the better option if he could swallow his pride in asking.

Marcus had done some investigating into the triad, and while they were very agreeable in lending or investing money, they were also harsh taskmasters when it came to getting their money back. Their offer of money was always accompanied by taking a large share of the profits and with a deadline. If the profits didn't come in as fast as they thought they should, they got their money in other ways. Marcus had seen articles about buildings burning down, people being hospitalized, and worse. Of course, it was never attributed to the triad, although their investment group was named as part owner of the establishments that had experienced losses. It was rumored that they took out heavy insurance policies on anything they had a part in and then if things didn't produce their desired results, there would be an insurance claim for millions of dollars when the company burned or the owner died.

Marcus didn't want that for David, but he didn't know how to convince him that borrowing some start up money from his father-in-law wouldn't be the end of the world.

David being out of the office was the ideal situation for Desi. She could make not so subtle passes at Marcus and not have to worry about potentially getting caught by the man who was supposedly her husband.

She was determined to get as much physical contact with him as she could. She hadn't missed the subtle way he looked at her cleavage when she unbuttoned her shirt lower than normal. Oh, he was trying to make it completely inconspicuous, but he wasn't succeeding. It was time to take the seduction up a notch.

Marcus was deep into the files that he had collected when he heard a knock at his door. Well, it wasn't really his door, since that was open, it was more at the door frame. He looked up to see Desi there. "I thought maybe you could use a break from all that tedious reading and chat for a bit." she said with a seductive smile. She walked over to his desk and stood behind his office chair. She began to massage his shoulders and the back of his neck. "Just as I suspected, the tension here is crazy. Let me help you relax."

Marcus knew that this was wrong, but it felt so amazing. He would stop her in a minute, he really did have some spots that could use her touch. His eyes were beginning to roll back into his head because this felt so good. He was practically falling asleep, he was feeling so relaxed.

Suddenly, falling asleep was the last thing on his mind. Desire had straddled herself across his lap and was massaging the back of his neck from her position in front of him. "Desi, what are you doing?" he exclaimed.

"Oh, come on now Marcus, you know what I'm doing." she purred into his ear. "I'm doing the thing both of us have been wanting to do for a long time."

"No, Desi, you're married." he objected.

"I'm married, I'm not dead. David is so consumed with this whole company that he doesn't even know I exist anymore. Please Marcus, I'm so lonely." she pleaded.

Marcus grabbed her wrists, he did it gently so that he wouldn't hurt her, but he pulled her hands away from his neck. "Desire, I'm sorry, I can't." He stood up helping to make sure she was balanced before he let her fully go.

"I understand, Marcus." she pouted. "I shouldn't have done that, like I said, I'm lonely, and you're such a sweet guy. I was hoping maybe we could be more than friends."

"I'm sorry, it's just not something that I am comfortable with." Marcus stated.

Desire had her head bowed as she walked out of his office. He wasn't sure if it was from shame or if she was disappointed. Either way, sending her on her way had been the right thing to do. He would admit though that for a few seconds there, having her on his lap had felt kind of nice. He wasn't sure how long he would be here, maybe trying to find someone to date wasn't a bad idea as long as he kept it from getting too deep. He would be leaving someday, and he didn't want to leave a woman that loved him. He might consider looking for something casual though.

Marcus got back to focusing on the task at hand. He knew he had entered the same search criteria into the bar so many times. He didn't know why he was still hoping for something new to come up on the list. Realizing that he was just wasting time going through the same list over and over again, he decided to call it a day and go home. Besides, with Desire sitting out there in the lobby, it was hard to focus anyway.

Desi made her way back to her desk with her head hanging low. Oh, she wasn't really sad about anything, however she needed to seem like she was if Marcus happened to follow her out of the office. She wasn't sad in the least.

She had felt the sign of his arousal. So, apparently, the lord of Paradise had made him physically human as well. He probably had no real clue what that all had meant, but it told her all she needed to know. She had a chance at completing her assignment, she just had to be persistent and not come across too strong, and also not back away from the challenge. She would succeed. She just had to keep wearing away and Marcus' resolve.

Chapter 7

Over the next several days, Marcus couldn't get Desi's proposition out of his mind. She hadn't given him an actual verbal proposition, although the implication was very obvious. Of course, it didn't help that she was right there every day when he went to work and she did everything she could to try to touch him. Oh, it wasn't as obvious as it had been that first day when she had sat on his lap, but it happened none the less. She needed to get past him in the break room. Although there was a whole other side to the table, she chose the one that he was on to walk past him. She made sure that she was close enough that her body slid across his as she passed.

He would be at the coffee maker pouring a cup of coffee and she needed to lean around him to grab something out of the cupboard. When she did, her whole upper body was pressed against his back. And of course, she acted like she couldn't find what she was looking for, so she had to stay against him and wiggle around while rummaging through the cupboard. He hadn't realized just how human he had been made because he couldn't help but feel aroused when she did that. He absolutely could not do anything about that. Her husband was his assignment. Not only would it cause a huge rift between him and David, it would not go well when the lord of Paradise found out about it. He tried his best to move away every time she did anything like that. It wasn't always easy.

The longer he worked for David though, the more he realized that there wasn't much he could do except try to convince the man that his father-in-law was really his best option. He began gathering all the information that he could about the triad. The problem was that it was never able to be proven that they had caused the 'accidents' or the loss of a business. The paper trail made anyone with an ounce of suspicion very sure what had happened, but they had never been charged with anything. They were smart men. They covered their steps well. Sure, there had been some speculation by others that they were a group to avoid, the question was, would David see the obvious trail, or would he just see it as a way to get the money he needed.

Maybe he could get Desire's help. Maybe she could introduce him so that he could talk to her father to see just what his terms would look like if David accepted his money. He would get a feel for whether or not the man was still willing to help out and if he was going to hold it over David's head. Marcus obviously had never had a family relationship, so he couldn't fully understand the dynamics that would be involved. He could understand a man wanting to have pride in the business that he had built and if someone else was going to undermine that it would be a hard pill to swallow.

Now, the problem was how to get Desi to want to introduce him to her father without it seeming like he was going behind David's back. Which, he totally was, although he didn't need anyone else to realize that. Maybe he should start showing interest in her. Or at least seem to show interest in her, not sexually, but maybe he could befriend her and then at some point tell her how much he would love to meet her father because he was a very savvy businessman.

The bigger problem though was, that he knew that he didn't really have a lot of time to work on a plan like that. He made his way out to the front office to see if Desi had any plans for lunch. David wasn't in the office anyway. He seemed to be spending a lot of time in the small lab he had built for himself at home. He was trying to get his product further along so it would be more attractive to potential investors. He needed the money before he could go into mass production, however if he could perfect the product, it might be more attractive to the people with the money to make it happen.

She seemed really excited that he would ask her. She quickly grabbed her purse and set the phones to the answering system. They didn't really get many calls though. No one knew who they were yet. She hooked her arm through his after she had locked up the main office door. They didn't bother with a sign that said when they would be back. No one really just showed up at the office expecting someone to be there.

"Where would you like to go?" Marcus asked.

"Oh, there's a really cozy café just a few blocks from here. Their food is amazing and it has such a warm atmosphere."

Desi said. They got into Marcus' car, and she directed him which way to go.

Marcus was a little surprised by the restaurant Desi had chosen. The first time they had gone to lunch she had picked someplace lavish. A place that she had probably gone to many times with her family. This place seemed more like David's style and definitely more in his price range.

"I like this place." he said. "You were right, it's very warm and cozy." He looked at the menu and saw things that one would likely suspect from a small friendly café like this one. There were soups and sandwiches. Probably things that most humans would look at as comfort food. They placed their order and Marcus noticed that Desi had chosen to sit next to him in the bench seat rather than across from him. Her body was pressed against him, it wasn't in a way that seemed super tight. He was just aware of her body being there. Of course, his attraction to her didn't help him to be able to ignore the proximity of her gorgeous curves and the smell of her body wash or perfume or whatever that was. He had to admit, Desi always smelled delicious.

Over their lunch, Marcus tried to make it seem as casual as he could, but he asked about her family. It was the best way he could think of to get to know as much as he could about her father. If he seemed interested in the man as a business icon, it wouldn't seem odd when he asked about meeting him some day.

In the end, it seemed like today was the perfect day to ask. Desi was obviously very infatuated with her father and his knowledge and skill in business. He didn't want to make it seem like a big deal though so he just stated casually, "I've seen your father's name in the business section of the papers and even in magazines. I have to admit his record is impressive. It seems almost like he had the Midas Touch when it comes to business."

"Oh, my daddy would like you." Desi said with a sparkle in her eye. "David seems to want to avoid my father at all costs. I understand him wanting to make his own name, but my daddy would help him if he could."

Two things became apparent to Marcus. Desi was very much a daddy's girl and convincing her father to invest in David's company would be so easy if David would just let it happen. Now, he just needed to wear David down on his aversion to having help from the man. He needed to get back to the conversation at hand though, so he said, "I'd love to meet him some day."

"Oh, that's easy, tomorrow we'll have lunch at the country club. My daddy's a member, and Wednesdays are his golf day. Not that he plays much golf. He sometimes gets in nine holes before moving inside to have lunch and cocktails." Desi said. "For him, it's really more about the schmooze. Many of his business associates are members there too, so they compare golf scores before they discuss business over a few martinis, sometimes more than a few actually." She had added that last part as if it were a thought that had just come to her from out of the air.

"Well, if David doesn't need me at the office, maybe we can have lunch there tomorrow." Marcus said.

"I'll let daddy know we might stop by." Desi said.

When they got back to the office, David still wasn't there, Desi had gone to check. Marcus could tell that it was bothering her to not have her husband ever be there and if he was working all the time while he was at home, it was going to be hard on their marriage. Actually, Marcus was pretty sure that it already was. He didn't think that Desi would be making moves on him if she weren't desperate and lonely. They were still basically newlyweds and she had obviously been in love with him at some point. Marcus was going to try to comfort her without going too far with it all.

That proved to be the hardest of his tasks though.

Desi always did her best to seem like she was really sad that David was never there with her. Honestly, she couldn't have cared less. David had nothing to do with her assignment, he was the one Marcus was sent here to save. She would never let Marcus see it because she didn't want him to realize that she was the reason that David didn't want to be around as much. She had started being really distant with him when they were at home. She was cold and calculating with him. The more it seemed like there could be trouble in the home, the more likely Marcus was to get over his self-righteousness and consider opening up to her. But she couldn't be the one to blame in his eyes. She had to be the poor deserted wife who deserved his attention and his sympathy.

She always made sure that Marcus knew that she was sad over not seeing David much lately. She complained about how she ended up going to bed alone most nights and she hadn't had any physical affection from him in a long while.

She had even gotten so good at this acting thing that she could summon up tears at will and had taken a few opportunities to cry on Marcus' shoulder. He had wrapped his arms around her and comforted her. He had tried to reassure her that it wouldn't be this way forever. David was just swamped with trying to get this product to market before anyone else did. He would be back to himself as soon as he did that.

"I don't think so Marcus, I think I've lost him forever." she wailed. "I'm so lonely, just hold me for a minute, the connection feels so good."

Marcus couldn't help but feel sorry for Desi and her situation with David. There wasn't really anything he could do about it though. He tried to cheer her up by reminding her that they were going to be meeting her father at his club today. That did make her smile, although her eyes still showed the pain of the feeling of rejection from her husband.

Chapter 8

They made their way to the country club just in time to find her father sitting waiting for them at the bar. Desi leaned in and kissed her father on the cheek. "Daddy, how was golfing today?"

"It went well, I got two under par, which isn't bad for half the course." he held her arms in his hands for a minute seeming to look at her for a minute. "You look stressed, baby girl. Is something going on?"

"Nothing I can't handle, daddy." she assured, "But if I find the need for help, you will be the first one I call."

She turned to toward Marcus slightly and said, "Daddy, this is Marcus. He's David's new personal assistant. He's read about you in the financials, and he was anxious to meet you."

Marcus held out his hand, "Mr. Davis, it's a pleasure to meet you. I've read so many good things in the papers about your business savvy and your philanthropic practices."

The man shook his hand and asked, "I've not heard your name before, are you from this area?"

"No, I moved here when David offered me the job as his assistant and I found the business plan intriguing." Marcus began. "I've always been in finance and this just seemed like the next logical step. I'm helping David with finding investors for the technology he's developing." Marcus wasn't going to admit that so far, there really wasn't any financing. No one had come on board. He didn't want to admit that at the first meeting though, that would be a betrayal to David. He was sure the man would step in and immediately offer to finance the entire project. Yes, it was likely that eventually he would ask the man for the money because there weren't other options, but he wasn't going to put it out there on the first meeting either.

"Well, I hope you can help him find what he needs. I want him to be successful after all, he's the one taking care of my baby girl." Kenneth said. "They are holding a table for us, can you stay for lunch?"

"That was the plan." Desi said with a huge smile.

Well, the man could have been worse, the fake Desi thought. This was the first time she had met him. Other than calling her baby girl, which was completely gross in her opinion, he probably seemed like an okay guy. She was sure that Marcus could tell that he was totally enamored with his daughter. From what she had read in the file, the real Desi had a huge daddy's girl complex, so she had to play along with that or he might become suspicious.

She wrapped one hand into the crook of Kenneth's arm and one into the crook of Marcus's arm and with all sweetness said, "I can't imagine how I got to be the lucky girl that has lunch with two such men."

Her plan was to lay it on thick with Marcus so that Kenneth would begin to doubt if her marriage was all that she had hoped it would be. She had no doubt that daddy dearest would be happy to give David the money if he would ask. The problem was, getting him to ask and that suited her just fine. If he took the money from the triad, Marcus' failed his assignment, and she had at least completed some of hers.

Marcus actually enjoyed the lunch with Kenneth. He wasn't at all overbearing or pretentious. He really would be the best option for David and the money he needed. If he could just get past his pride and ask.

After they had ordered their meals, Kenneth said, "Tell me more about yourself."

Fortunately, Marcus had been given a back story to share with anyone that might ask. "Well, I'm originally from Dallas. My family still lives there."

"Desi hasn't told me your last name, would you have any connections that I might recognize?" Kenneth asked.

"Well, may name is Johnson, so it's pretty common all around the country. I'm not sure if I'm related to anyone that you know." Marcus said. He had been told that was exactly why he had been given a rather ambiguous name, no one would think he was related to someone they already had connections with, or if they did, it would be easy to correct them as needed.

Desi didn't change her flirtatious ways at all simply because her father was there with them. Although, her father didn't seem at all upset by that. Maybe he was just used to his daughter flirting with men who weren't her husband. Or he liked Marcus better for some reason.

The man was still hung up on the name. "Yes, Johnson is a fairly common name. Do you know any of the corporations or businesses your family is involved with in Texas?"

Oh, this was not going to bode well, He didn't know anyone else named Johnson, he wasn't technically named Johnson. It was a made up name, but he had to say something. It wasn't like it could be checked, if he claimed some distant relative somewhere. "I know that I'm related to the baby company. You know the shampoo and all that. I'm just not sure exactly how I'm related to them, I've never met any of them, I do know that there's a connection in there somewhere."

"Oh, well, that's fine stock to have come from." Kenneth said.

Maybe Marcus should have aimed lower. He didn't want the man thinking that he was wealthy or had some high connections. "True, but as I said, I don't really know that part of the family." he hedged. Desi could obviously see his distress, she came to his rescue.

"Oh, daddy." she scolded. "It's the twenty-first century; people don't talk about coming from 'stock' anymore. The way this world is, people don't have to come from any specific family to make a name for themselves and be successful. Marcus is a self-made man and he's doing a lot to help David at the office."

The man didn't look as if his daughter's words had taken any of the wind out of his sails. He would leave the topic alone for now, Marcus had no doubt that at some point the topic would come back up again if he was here on Earth long enough to spend much time with the man across the table from him.

"I have to say, sir, that I've read a lot of articles about you and your business dealings, and I'm impressed. You seem to have the Midas touch as they say." Marcus was trying to make the man focus more on himself than on who Marcus may or may not be related to.

"Well, thank you." the older man began. "Please, call me Kenneth, sir is far too formal. Anyone who is a friend of Desi's needs to feel comfortable with me."

"Kenneth it is then." Marcus said.

"So what project are you working on at the moment?" Kenneth asked.

Marcus wasn't really sure what to say to that. He couldn't exactly tell the man what he was doing because he was actively trying to help David in his desire to avoid telling the man that he needed money.

"Daddy, must we talk about business all the time. I want to hear about your trip to the Hamptons last week. I'm sure it was amazing." Desi said. Marcus was relieved to have her change the topic. He wondered if she had done it intentionally to save him from having to say things he wasn't supposed to be saying.

"Well, if you think it was so amazing, why didn't you go with us. You know all of your old friends keep asking when you're going to join us for a week or even a weekend."

"I know daddy. I really will try to get up there sometime soon, maybe Labor Day weekend. It's just that David has been so busy with work that we haven't really had a chance to get away." Desi explained.

"Well, you have been married almost two years now. I'm sure he could manage a few days without you at his beck and call every minute of every day. You really should take a break from life in the city. It would do you a world of good." her father argued. "If David can't get away, that doesn't mean that you can't have a short trip and catch up with old friends."

"I know daddy, I'll try, I really will." She sounded exasperated. Marcus was sure this wasn't the first time her father had pushed for this and he was just as sure that it wouldn't be the last time either.

Marcus tried to derail the man from putting so much pressure on Desi. He didn't want to change the topic completely that would seem odd. "The Hamptons, I've heard so many good things, but I've never been. Do you have a house on the coast?"

"We do, it's divided into two wings, one is mainly for family, the other for guests. Six bedrooms in each wing, and a guest house further down the property. We also have a staff quarters behind the eight stall garage." Kenneth said with pride. "If I can ever talk Desi into making the trip again, maybe you can come with her. David obviously isn't interested."

"Well, I'll keep that in mind." Marcus said. He wasn't going to sound overly enthused about going when it was something that was obviously something David had some reason to not want to engage in. He wondered if the family was as happy as they wanted everyone to think they were. Sometimes wealthy people had more than their share of internal conflict. Money wasn't always the answer to everything.

"Daddy, I think you embarrassed Marcus, he barely even knows us and you're inviting him to a weekend in the Hamptons. Give him a chance to see who we are." Desi scolded.

"Seems I can't say anything right today." the man grumbled. "I can't get to know Marcus, but I shouldn't invite him to the beach house until I know him better. Which is it Desi?" He didn't seem angry it was more like frustration at getting thwarted at every topic he tried to discuss.

"Oh, daddy. That's not true. Why don't you tell Marcus about your company. He's interested in business and finance. I'm sure he'd love to hear all about how you got started and where you are now." Desi said trying to soothe her father.

While Marcus wasn't overly interested in the man's business beyond what he had read in the financials in the paper and on the Internet, he could see that the man completely lit up when he was allowed to talk so freely about something that meant so much to him.

Desi was careful to not be overly obvious about her flirtation with Marcus. She wasn't sure exactly what Kenneth would think of her making advances on her husband's assistant. Although, from what she had read in the files, he likely wasn't an overly loyal man. There were rumors of affairs with both employees and household staff. However, she also knew that some men didn't believe that what was good for the gander was also good for the goose. Some men found it their right to have affairs while they expected their wives to be completely loyal. That was a double standard that Desi didn't agree with. She still kept her flirtation to simple brushes of his hand and a small stroke on his thigh.

Movements that wouldn't seem obvious to the older man, but definitely enough to keep Marcus attuned to her.

She wasn't sure how much longer they were going to be on Earth, so she needed to up her game and try to seduce him sooner rather than later. She knew he was interested, he just had to get past that whole morals thing where he wasn't willing to go against her marriage vows. Maybe if he thought that David was being unfaithful he might be more willing to consider an affair. She decided to go for it and make her move.

"Daddy." she said softly. "I wanted to talk to you about something. I'm afraid that David is being unfaithful, I don't have any proof, but it just seems likely. He's never around, he doesn't come into the office hardly at all. When I go home at night, he's either not there, or he's locked away in that lab of his. I just don't know what to do." She actually had managed to manufacture a few tears. She took her napkin and dabbed at her eyes.

Kenneth looked as though he almost had steam coming out of his ears at her statement. "I'll kill him!" he growled.

"No, daddy, like I said, I'm not sure it's just making me so lonely to never have him around. I don't know what to do." she took that opportunity to bury her face into the crook of Marcus' shoulder and fake cry.

Marcus wasn't exactly sure what to do other than to draw Desi into him and let her cry. He looked at her father to see what his reaction was.

The man gave a brief nod as if he understood something, what it was, Marcus had no clue. After a minute, he spoke. "Marcus, it's obvious that she feels comfortable with you. She wouldn't have spoken so freely with you here if she didn't. I know that I have no right to ask this favor, but I'd appreciate it if you would be her friend and spend time with her until I can get this whole thing sorted out and figure out what is going on with her husband. I know that I have no right to ask this, it's just that she means the world to me and I can't bear to see her this unhappy. I'll gladly pay for your time if that's what it takes for you to agree."

Marcus was surprised by the man's plea, although maybe he shouldn't have been, he could tell that Desi was everything to him. Marcus really didn't think that David was having an affair, but he had to admit that he couldn't be sure. He did like Desi. "I'll look after her for a while, until things get figured out. And you don't need to pay me, I have become her friend too and I couldn't take money from you just to keep her company for a few days."

Marcus felt Desi shift and soon, her arm was wrapped around his neck and she kissed him on the cheek. "Oh, thank you Marcus, thank you so much. I don't know what I would do without you."

The older man stayed a short time longer just to make sure that his daughter was back on solid footing emotionally and then he excused himself because he had business to attend to. Marcus was pretty sure that business included hiring a private investigator or someone who would get to the bottom of Desi's accusations.

When they arrived at David and Desi's house, the house appeared quiet with no cars in the driveway. Desi paused for a minute and then took a deep breath. "I can't bare to go in there alone. Marcus, would you come in for coffee or take me to a coffee shop or, oh, I don't know, anything. I just don't want to spend another entire night sitting alone in a quiet house."

Marcus didn't feel right about going into David's house with Desi. If the man came home, he might assume that something was going on between the two of them and that wouldn't be a good idea if he was still going to try to work with David and convince him to take the money from a safe source.

Apparently, he hesitated too long, because Desi started to open her door and said, "Never mind, forget I said anything." She started to get out of the car.

Marcus put a hand on her arm to stop her. "No, Desi, wait. It's not that I don't want to hang out with you. I'm just not sure that doing that here is the best option. If David is cheating, you don't want to be here when he gets home, and if he isn't cheating, I shouldn't be here when he gets home because then it might look like you are the one that is cheating. I was just going to suggest that maybe we go back to my apartment so we don't have to worry about it either way."

Desi sat back more solidly in her seat and smiled. "I think that's a good idea, Marcus. Thank you for being such a good friend." And hopefully much more than a friend soon, Desi thought to herself.

Marcus drove to his apartment, it wasn't huge, but it did have two bedrooms, so if Desi needed a place to sleep, he could provide that for her. He wasn't sure exactly how long she was wanting to stay. If it were for more than one night, she would probably need to go home and get clothes and toiletries for herself. While his shower gel and other products weren't overly masculine, they weren't very feminine either. He hoped that her father could get to the bottom of things quickly though. Having Desi here in his space was going to be a challenge to his already tenuous resolve to not fall for her and her advances.

He offered her some coffee, she declined and asked if he had any wine. He actually did, he just wasn't sure that was a good idea for him and his ability to remain steadfast to being nothing more than a friend to her. She could have a glass though, she probably needed one after the kind of day she had had.

Chapter 9

After they had eaten the Chinese food they ordered for dinner, Marcus tried to figure out a way to not be too close to Desi. He would not be rude, however if they could find something to do that would distract them both, it would be a good thing. "Hey, want to watch a movie or play a game?" he asked. "I don't have a ton of games, I have a few. I have all the good channels on the television."

"Sure, we can Netflix and chill." Desi said with a smile.

Marcus wasn't sure what that phrase meant, but he did have Netflix, so he opened it up on his television and handed the remote to Desi to pick something that she wanted to watch. He regretted that decision when she picked something that was very erotic and steamy. It wasn't porn, however it was about as close as anything could get without being banned from the channel.

Desi knew exactly what she was doing, she picked one of the steamiest movies she knew of. She was determined to get Marcus to at least fool around a little. It would be great if he would go all in and take her to bed. But she wasn't sure she could get him to that point this quickly. Even if they could have a steamy make out session or some light petting, it would be a step to where she needed them to go.

Marcus didn't have a lot of furniture. That made sense since he had just moved here, and he was single. That played to her advantage. They had to sit together on his couch. There weren't any other seats that could see the television.

She started out a polite distance away from him, but she slowly moved closer. It wasn't obvious, she would just lean a little and then shift and her body ended up closer to his than it had been a few minutes ago. A few times of doing that and she could feel the heat of his body radiating onto her arm.

Another move like that and she was brushing her breast against his arm. He tried to shift away, however he had originally sat as close to the armrest as he could to give her space so he didn't have very far to move. When the movie got to a particularly hot scene, she put her hand on his thigh and said, "This has always been one of my favorite parts of this movie. It's so romantic. Like you can tell that he is so into her, and she's just as into him. I bet he would never consider having an affair behind her back." She added that last part to try to remind him that she had every right to not be completely devoted to her husband at this point.

She could tell that her actions were making Marcus uncomfortable, but wasn't that what she needed to do in order to cause him to stumble. Her two goals were to make him fail in his attempt to keep David on the right path with his business and who he got to finance it, and to take

Marcus down by corrupting his own moral standards. She wasn't sure there was a lot that she could do as far as the financial aspect. She could try to convince David to take the money from Kenneth, but she wasn't sure that he would listen to her. On the other hand, she knew just how to tempt a man into wanting her. She had been given the body of a beautiful woman. If he had been given a mostly human body, her actions would be hard to resist. From the reactions he was having, she was pretty sure that he had a body that was either fully or at least predominantly human. He was squirming and trying to shift his pants away from his arousal.

She allowed her hand to slowly climb higher up his leg, almost as if she didn't even realize she had done it. Soon, the side of her hand was right beside his dick and balls.

Marcus tried to stand up with an excuse of getting them some snacks to munch on, but Desi halted his progress. "Oh, Marcus, I'm not really hungry. That Chinese food really filled me up. She was lying, she had always found that Chinese food went through her system faster than it really should. She wasn't going to tell him that though.

"Can you just hold me for a bit?" she asked trying to sound as timid as possible. "This movie always makes me think of being in love and being with someone you care about. Right now, with David having an affair, I just need someone to give me some comfort and be my friend." The thing was, David wasn't having an affair. She was pretty sure that he had sensed something different about his wife so he was trying to avoid her until he figured out what to do. That didn't stop Marcus from offering her comfort though. She knew this wasn't going to be a speedy process, she also knew she only had until David made a move one way or another with the triad and their offer of funding. She had to move quickly, she also needed to be smart about it. If she came on too strong, he would run in the other direction, but if she could feed his empath side, she might just have a chance.

She felt Marcus put his arm around her, although it was stiff and awkward, he was trying not to really touch her while offering her comfort. She took hold of his hand and pulled it more tightly around her. The fact that it ended up with his hand on her breast was just a bonus. She snuggled into him, pressing her body tightly against him. She sat like that for several minutes before stretching up to place a kiss on his cheek. "Thank you for this Marcus, I just feel so alone and so lost. Being here with you is so nice." She used her hand to turn his face toward her and she leaned up and placed her lips on his. At first, he was stiff and not participating in the kiss at all, the more she moved her mouth slowly, the more he responded.

Marcus could feel the awkwardness of the kiss, was that because he knew he shouldn't be doing it, or was that because he had never kissed anyone before? He wasn't sure, so he let Desi take the lead. He really did like kissing her. He shouldn't, but he did. She tasted sweet. That may have been from the wine she had been drinking, or it may have just been her natural taste. He didn't know much about these things.

He put his arms more fully around Desi and drew her more tightly to him. She shifted so that she was straddling his lap. He could feel heat radiating from her pussy onto his body. His cock reacted in the way he was sure any man's would. It began to thicken and harden, it was becoming uncomfortable in his boxer briefs, especially with Desi pressed so tightly against it.

He lifted her slightly so that his cock had room to move. There was no way that she wasn't feeling his arousal. They kissed for a long time, their tongues swirling, their bodies moving against each other. It felt amazing.

And then, Marcus had a moment of clarity and realized just what he was doing. He pulled Desi away from him and lifted her as he stood. He made sure she was steady on her feet and then he stepped back. "I'm sorry, Desi. We shouldn't be doing this, you're a married woman."

Desi lowered her eyes and contritely said, "You're right, I'm sorry. I'll go to bed now." She walked away to go to the room Marcus had shown her earlier.

Damn it all! Desi thought to herself. It wasn't the outcome she had hoped to have tonight, but it was better than nothing. For a brief moment, when Marcus had started to stand up, she had hoped that he was taking her to his bedroom. When he had pushed her away, her hopes had fallen.

She was sure that he wouldn't be able to keep his resolve forever, but she wasn't sure how much time they both had left on Earth.

The following day, Desi was in Marcus's office flirting with him, she was sitting on his desk right in front of him when they heard the main office door open. Desi quickly darted into the space under the desk and told Marcus "If it's David, tell him I stepped out to do some shopping."

Marcus tried to look as nonchalant as possible with a woman under his desk. He heard David call out for his wife from the front of the office. He looked into the office and said "Do you know where Desi is? I didn't see her anywhere."

"She said something about stepping out to do some shopping." Marcus said. He was trying to keep his voice normal but Desi was making that difficult. She was running her hands on his upper thigh, coming very close to his balls.

"Oh." David said, He did sound disappointed in not finding her, but he made his way down to his office.

As soon as Desi heard David close his office door, she reached up and unzipped the fly to his pants. He tried to stop her hand, but she was determined. And admittedly, maybe he was enjoying her touch, even though he knew that he shouldn't.

Desi worked her hand inside of his pants and caressed his hardening cock through his boxer briefs. She was rather cramped being under his desk, but she couldn't risk having her head bob out and take the risk that David would see her. She knew that Marcus would be very upset and never be alone with her again if David had any idea of what was going on.

After she had stroked him long enough that she could tell he was going to have an orgasm soon. She would have put her mouth over the tip of his cock, but that would require her lifting her head above the level of the desk. Which wouldn't bother her, she didn't care who might see what was going on, but Marcus would. Especially with David right down the hall.

"Grab some tissue." Desi said. She knew Marcus would have no clue that what was about to happen could be very messy and possibly make his pants need a thorough washing.

At first Marcus hesitated, not understanding the command. He grabbed a small bundle of the tissues, but kept the box right in front of him on the desk in case he needed more. It didn't take many more seconds and he began to understand the need for them. He did his best to keep the semen on the tissues, grabbing more as needed. After the orgasm was over, he felt very odd. He felt extreme pleasure physically, but mentally, he was warring with himself. He knew this was wrong, but he couldn't honestly say that he was positive he could keep it from happening again.

When his legs weren't vibrating, he stood up and made himself decent before walking over to shut his office door. He closed it quietly hoping that David wouldn't hear it through his own closed door. When the door was closed, he turned to help Desi out from under his desk, but she had managed that on her own. She was brushing her pants to make sure there wasn't any debris on them and then straightened her blouse.

Desi looked at Marcus with a smile. "That was amazing." she said.

"I agree" Marcus said. "Although I don't really understand what about that was amazing for you. I believe I received all the pleasure."

"Physically, yes." Desi agreed. "But I have needed someone to give pleasure to for a while now and it felt great to do so." She really was good at this, she sounded like the poor neglected wife who had love she just wanted to give somebody.

"We really shouldn't have done that though." Marcus said.

Desi immediately put her head down and acted like the poor rejected girl. "I know, Marcus." she said softly. "I have just been so lonely. I know I shouldn't have done that. It's not your fault at all. I took advantage of you."

Marcus could see that Desi was close to crying over his statement. He didn't want to hurt her or reject her more than she already felt, but this really shouldn't be happening. "It's okay, Desi. It wasn't something either of us planned to have happen. We just need to be more diligent about it in the future."

"Of course." Desi said with a nod.

Chapter 10

David looked up and saw the three men that called themselves Dynacorp. He didn't think they had ever given him their real names. He had taken to calling them Huey, Lewie, and Dewey in his own mind just to keep them straight. It seemed like Huey was usually the one that talked the most. The other two seemed to mostly be there to enforce the belief that they were a group of investors that took risks on smaller start-ups if they felt that they could be profitable.

"We just wanted to get back with you, David." Huey began. "We haven't heard from you in a while and we're really looking forward to getting this project started. We need to get your stuff out there before anyone else figures out how to do what you are doing."

"I know." David said. "I'm just trying to consider all my options. I don't want to make the wrong decision when it comes to my business. I need this to be able to support me and my family for the foreseeable future.

"David, David, David." Huey said. "You're never going to get a better offer than we gave you. We only want a thirty percent interest for our investment. We will be hands off, we don't want to interfere, you know what you're doing with the technology. We just want to invest in an up and coming business where we foresee unlimited potential."

The other two men seemed to be pressing in a little more as if to make a united front. David wasn't sure if it was meant to intimidate him or not, however it certainly did. He didn't want to take money from these men because of the rumors he had heard, on the other hand, he didn't have a whole lot of other options. "I'll make my decision by the end of the month. I swear."

That seemed to be enough for them for now. They left, but Lewie and Dewey both looked back at him with a look that was quite menacing.

The more he talked to them, the more he really felt like taking money from them wasn't a good idea, the problem was, could he swallow his pride and talk to his father-in-law.

The day after the office orgasm, Desi told Marcus that she just couldn't bare going to work right now, she was going to stay home and call in sick. Let David wonder where his own wife was. It served him right. That's what she told Marcus anyway. She texted David and told him that she had decided to spend a few days or so with some of her college friends. She told him that she totally understood that he was super busy and loaded down with work right now. She wasn't upset with him, but she felt like it would be better for both of them if she just took a few days away to catch up with old friends. She told him that she had told Marcus that she wasn't feeling well because she didn't feel she needed to explain herself to a lowly employee. That should keep the two of them from talking about her absence from work for a few days.

Then, she set about her seduction of Marcus. When he got home that evening, she planned to have a dinner by candlelight and some good wine to get him relaxed and hopefully in the mood for her to make some moves on him that would hopefully have him ready to take her to his bed, or the bed in the guest room, the location didn't really matter, as long as she got him to be crazy with need to have sex with her.

David had texted Marcus to tell him that he was going to be out of the office all day and trying to set up some meetings with investors and working in the lab. That was probably a good idea, that way Marcus wouldn't have to try to explain Desi's absence. Hopefully she had contacted him to let him know what was going on. Well, not what was going on fully, but the fact that she was taking time off of work. He needed to figure out how to avoid her, so he didn't give into temptation.

He decided to work as long as he could, until he got a text from her asking when he would be home. She had prepared a really nice dinner to thank him for letting her stay with him for a while and she needed to know when to put it in the oven.

He couldn't leave her hanging after she had gone to so much effort to make a nice meal for him. Avoiding her wasn't going to be possible while she was staying at his home. Maybe he could encourage her to go back home and be there when David did return home.

He walked into his place, and the smell was amazing. He didn't know what Desi had cooked, but she was obviously really good at it.

She came out from the kitchen and Marcus had to admit that wasn't an outfit that he would have pictured most women wanting to spend much time in the kitchen cooking in. It was form fitting and wrapped around her like a glove. The front was cut low enough that it showed an ample amount of her cleavage. If it had gone much lower, he would have been able to see her navel. He was in so much trouble. Even if he could somehow manage to not follow through on the thoughts in his mind and the things his body was telling him he should do, he had already lusted after her far more than he should have.

"Marcus, you're home. Here let me take your coat." She helped him remove his coat and went to put it over the back of a chair near the door. "I opened a bottle of wine to let it breathe, would you mind doing the honors and pouring?"

"Of course." Marcus said. Seeing her from the back wasn't much help to his libido either. That dress hugged every curve of her gorgeous body. There was no mistaking her small waist that accentuated how full her ass was. It gave him the overwhelming urge to put both hands on her and squeeze like he was checking to see if the melon was ripe. He knew she was in good shape, so it would be firm, but not so firm that he couldn't sink his fingers into her flesh.

"Marcus, here, let me help you with your jacket." she purred. Instead of going around behind him, like most would to help, she ran her hands up his pectorals and slid it off of his shoulders. That put her right in front of him, and really close. He could smell her scent, one that he had come to know was part body wash, and part Desi herself. No matter what time of day it was, she had a special scent that was completely hers. It was intoxicating to him, he couldn't help himself, he leaned in to take a deeper inhale. He had closed his eyes so that he could concentrate on the wonderful aroma which left him vulnerable for her to lean up and kiss him.

He didn't pull away, so she deepened the kiss and soon, their tongues were doing a tango of sorts, moving from his mouth to hers. One would draw back a little, and the other would pursue. Soon, Marcus heard his jacket fall to the floor and Desi wrapped her arms around him, one had playing at the bottom of his hairline and the other holding tightly to his neck. Her body was pressed as closely to his as it could be with them both standing and the height difference. He wrapped his hands around her, at the waist to start, he couldn't help but run one hand down to cup her luscious ass.

Desi seemed like she was almost trying to climb up his body. He placed his other hand on her ass and lifted her into him. His cock craved the warmth of her pressed tightly against it through his slacks. She moved herself against his hard cock and even through the material, it felt amazing. Obviously, it was something he had never experienced before, but it was beyond amazing. He knew he shouldn't be doing this, however he couldn't help himself.

This is it, Desi thought to herself. I'm going to take him down and get some pleasure for myself in the process. She ground her pelvis into him as hard as she could against his rigid dick. It was arousing her and it was definitely arousing him.

She reached between them, which wasn't exactly easy, because they were so tightly pressed together. She pulled her lower body far enough away that she could unbuckle his belt and unfasten his pants. He just kept kissing her. He definitely didn't seem like he wanted her to stop her actions.

When she had his pants completely unfastened, she reached in to free his cock. She wrapped her hands around the hard shaft and began to stroke him. "Marcus, you're so hard and your cock is so big." She really didn't know what size it was compared to anyone else but giving him an ego boost would never be a bad thing.

"Let's go to the bedroom." she requested.

For whatever reason, that was what broke his concentration enough that he pushed her away. "I'm sorry, Desi, this isn't right. Like I said yesterday, we both have to make a better effort to avoid this." He refastened his slacks and belt and said "Let's just enjoy the wonderful meal you've prepared, it smells amazing."

Desi was disappointed, however, she wasn't going to let this stop her from trying again. Which was exactly why she had set the table so that she sat on the side and he sat at the head. Most would think that two people setting at a table they would sit opposite, she wanted to be able to touch him.

When the food was all on the table, she took a moment to pause and grasp his hand. "Marcus, I'm sorry if I was too forward, please forgive me. I'm just so lonely." She gave his hand a tight squeeze.

"It's okay, Desi." Marcus said softly. "I do understand, it's just not something that we should do is all."

"I know, but I can't help myself. You're so handsome and to be honest, David and I haven't been intimate in months. Even before all of this financing stuff started, he was distant. Honestly, I don't remember the last time we made love." That was all true. She hadn't ever been intimate with David, so it wasn't a lie to say it had been a long time. She wasn't the real Desi, so of course she hadn't had sex with David. And although she probably could have sex with him now because he thought she was his wife. She had no interest in that though. Marcus was her only desire and that wasn't so much about him physically, it was about the goal to corrupt him.

She didn't want to push him too much more right now, since he had just told her no, but she wasn't going to completely back off either. She made sure that when she passed something to him, their hands brushed against each other. A few times, she intentionally let her bare foot rub his ankle under his slacks. Nothing long and lasting, just a brief touch here and there. She could tell it was affecting him, although he was trying really hard to act like it wasn't. He shifted in his seat frequently, trying to make it seem nonchalant, but it totally wasn't. When she could get a glimpse of the front of his slacks, he was still at least semi hard.

Marcus was extremely uncomfortable. He had seen the near tears in Desi's eyes when he had told her no earlier and the last thing that he wanted to do was make her cry, it was just that he knew that he shouldn't be going down that path. Although, he really wanted to.

Could he have a brief affair with her while he was here, if David never found out about it? Of course, the lord of Paradise would know about it, but if it didn't affect the outcome for David and his business, was it really breaking the rules? He was trying to convince himself that it wouldn't really be a bad thing because he was just offering comfort and support to a woman who was in obvious pain over being rejected by her husband.

He knew that was a baseless argument, it was still wrong, but what they had done so far was amazing. He wanted to know more, he wanted to have more.

Desi knew that now wasn't the time to push. She could back off at least long enough for them to enjoy dinner. She set about getting the meal plated and on the table. She would still make subtle physical contact, a brush of her hand over his when reaching for something. Her foot 'accidently' brushed over his from time to time. They didn't really say much during the meal other than what was needed to pass food. Marcus had told her the meal was as delicious as it had smelled when he came in.

The sexual tension between them was almost like a current running through a wire. There was an almost crackle in the air.

Marcus wasn't sure what to say or do as he helped Desi clear the table. He had to figure out his own inner battle before he could have the words to say to her. He had to think of something else to do to try to keep them busy.

"Hey, you picked the movie the last time." he began, "This time it's my turn." He would pick out something so sweet and clean that it at least wouldn't make their situation any worse. He still only had the couch that faced the TV. It would seem odd if he tried to move the recliner over to where he could see the television. So he sat on one end of the couch.

He was surprised when she sat most of the way down the couch. He was sure she would sit right next to him.

Desi was sure that Marcus was surprised that she sat so far away. She had a motive for that though. After the movie got started and they had sat apart for a while. About fifteen minutes into the movie, Desi stretched and laid down with her head in Marcus's lap. She felt him tense under her, but he didn't push her away. She just laid there for a while, allowing him to get used to it and relax.

The movie was almost half over before she felt like his body was no longer protesting. She twisted more so that her face was close enough that all she had to do was turn her head and she would be in a position to take him in her mouth. Of course, his pants were still between them. She would have to figure out a way to work around that. She put her hand under her cheek, just like someone would on a pillow. That allowed her to start caressing his cock through his pants. It was just a brush here and there to start with.

As he began to get aroused, Desi upped her game and started to brush against him with the intent of making him harder. It worked.

She turned her body so that she could more easily access his fly and she unzipped him. She knew most would move slowly so that she didn't pressure him, but that didn't fit into her plan of making him completely fall for her and her advances.

She removed his cock from the confines and was pleased to see him lift his hips a little so that she could gain access more easily. When she had him freed from the fabric, she encircled him with her mouth, licking him with her tongue. She slid her mouth up and down his hard shaft and used one hand at the base to hold him firmly and one hand to fondle his balls. She worked her head up and down, altering between quick bobs and long slow draws. She swirled her tongue around and always made sure to lick the sensitive underside just below the tip. She was happy to see that the Lord of Paradise had definitely made him look exactly like a real human male. She knew how to please them.

Marcus needed to tell her to stop, he really did. He just couldn't. Although a part of him did want her to stop so that he could do something that would give her pleasure too. He wasn't sure exactly what that was, but he felt like this should be give and take.

"Tell me how I can make you feel as good as you are making me feel." he said. That sounded okay, right? It didn't sound like he was a total novice who had done none of this before, it sounded like a man who wanted to give the woman pleasure in the way that she liked best.

Desi totally knew that Marcus had no clue what to do, so she didn't want to try to engage in anything too complicated. She would love to have him do oral on her, but it probably wouldn't be all that enjoyable anyway since he had never done it before and it would totally ruin the experience for her if she was having to give him step by step instructions on exactly how to do it. Besides, the sooner she could get him to have actual intercourse with her, the sooner her goal of corrupting him completely would be accomplished.

"I just want you inside of me." she said panting. "Please Marcus, I don't care if you're on top or if I am, I just need to feel you inside of me." She thought maybe he would have her be on top because he wouldn't know what to do, but it seemed like pure animal lust had taken over and he told her to lay back on the couch.

She removed her clothing quickly before laying back with her legs spread so that Marcus had full access to her. She didn't think this would be a super satisfying experience physically, but the satisfaction of getting him to fall from grace would be well worth putting up with a less than ideal physical experience.

Marcus paused before just climbing on top of Desi. He had never seen a naked woman before other than a few in movies on HBO. He took a brief pause to admire her. "You are so beautiful, Desi." he said. "I've never seen such a beautiful woman." He knew that he could say that because she wouldn't know that he had never seen a real woman before. She would think that she was comparing him to others that he had seen in the past.

"On second thought." Marcus said. He leaned over to scoop Desi up and carried her down the hall to his bedroom. He was going to do his best to make this experience good for both of them. He already had no clue what he was supposed to be doing. He didn't want to add having to try to balance on the couch to the maneuver. He laid her out before undressing himself and then laid down beside her.

He took the opportunity to touch and caress her body. She was so soft. He was getting more and more aroused as he explored her body. He wouldn't be able to hold out much longer. The voice in the back of his head telling him this was a huge mistake didn't go away, he just refused to listen to it.

Desi leaned up and placed her mouth over his. She pulled him closer to her. "Marcus, please, I need you inside of me."

Hearing those words, Marcus couldn't wait any longer, he leveraged himself over Desi and slowly eased himself into her. He wasn't sure if a woman enjoyed a slower entry or if they preferred something more rapid. He didn't want to go too fast though, he wanted to savor every second of the experience. He slid his cock in and out a few times slowly, trying to go as deep as he could possibly go. The feeling of her heat wrapped around him was almost too much. He wanted to go harder and faster, but he was also afraid that would end things too quickly. It was his first time having sex after all. He wanted this to last.

After a few minutes of letting them both acclimate to the new sensations, Desi said, "More Marcus. I need you harder and faster. You feel so good inside of me."

Marcus wouldn't argue with that request. He wanted the same thing. He hoped he wasn't crushing Desi. He tried to keep his upper body from having his full weight on her, but he just couldn't help wanting to be so tightly pressed against her that they seemed almost like one.

It took longer than Desi had thought it might for Marcus to come. With it being his first time, she thought it might be what humans referred to as a quickie. Most likely, the hand job she had given him at the office had at least made him last a little bit longer.

Marcus kissed Desi deeply before moving himself off of her and excusing himself. He went into the restroom and took care of business. He didn't know exactly what to do, but for some reason, it seemed like he should clean up the mess he had just made. He got a warm wet washcloth and took it to clean Desi's pussy. He wiped her gently. He didn't know for sure if what they had done left a woman tender or sore and he didn't want to take any chance on causing her irritation.

"That's so sweet of you Marcus." Deis purred. "I've never had a man take care of me this way before. You're such a kind and gentle lover."

Marcus wasn't sure what to say to that. He was just doing what seemed like the right thing to do. He had no clue what other men did. "I just want to take care of you, Desi. I feel like I used you or took advantage of you."

"Nonsense, Marcus." she said. "You did exactly what we both wanted to do. I've been hoping this would happen for a while now and our first time was perfect."

Marcus took the washcloth back to the bathroom and returned to snuggle with Desi. He had seen movies that said that women liked to snuggle after sex. They ended up falling asleep in each other's arms.

Chapter 11

Desi pleaded with Marcus, "Please go with me to the Hamptons. My parents won't be there and I'll be all alone. Well, except for the staff, but that's not the same thing."

"Why don't you ask David." Marcus suggested. "I'm sure he could use a weekend away from all that's going on for him right now."

"Oh, I did ask him, and he just blew it off." She totally had not asked him, but she didn't want Marcus to know that or have any way of figuring it out. "He pretty much got upset with me for even asking. He said that I know that he is too busy right now and that he didn't want to hear anything more about it." That should keep him from butting in if he did see David.

"I just don't think it's a good idea for us to go away together." Marcus debated.

"Oh, please, I need to get out of this city for a few days and I don't want to go alone. I'll just sit and think about everything that is going on with David if I'm left to myself for so many hours." Desi said. "It will be fun, I promise. We can totally just chill and have the cook make us amazing food, or we can go out and get some amazing seafood. Whatever you want to do. Just don't make me do it all alone."

Marcus knew he should stay firm and not go with her, but he was falling for her more and more all the time. He knew that what he was feeling for her was not supposed to be happening, but he couldn't help himself. He wanted her very much physically and he cared about her happiness. He could tell that she was so unhappy being ignored so much by David. If her parents were going to be there, he would totally encourage her to go with them and have some time to just be away from it all, but apparently, they had some charity function over the weekend that they had to attend and it was in the opposite direction of the Hamptons.

Desi could tell that Marcus was really not in favor of the idea, but she also knew that the quickest way to get him to agree to anything was for her to appear sad and dejected. "I understand." she said with tears in her eyes. She had gotten really good at being able to summon up those tears.

Marcus couldn't remain strong very well when Desi started to cry. That got to him every time. He couldn't do anything except agree to go to the Hamptons with her. "Okay, when do we leave?" he asked.

She told him that there would be a car waiting for them within the hour. He hadn't expected it to all happen quite that fast. Marcus went to his room to pack a suitcase. He wasn't sure exactly what he would need for a long weekend in the Hamptons, so he just made sure that he had an assortment of things, both casual and dressy as well as his swimsuit and toiletries.

Desi had taken the opportunity of her parents not being able to go to the Hamptons that weekend to make sure that she and Marcus would have plenty of time alone and away from the city. It might be easier to get Marcus to let down his guard for more contact with her. He had already gotten more into the idea than she had thought he might at first and she was hoping that she could push him for more while they were gone.

When her father had offered his limo to take them to the large home on the beach, she had readily accepted. So far, she hadn't gotten much physical satisfaction as she would have liked to have, but she had a plan for that to change. She had chosen to wear a somewhat flowy dress that had a slit on the one side. It was low cut enough to show an adequate amount of cleavage and when she moved just right, it gave a glimpse of her leg. She hadn't worn any underwear, that would have just messed with her plan.

They stepped out of the house and as Desi's father had promised, his limo was waiting for them and the driver was standing patiently waiting to open the door for them. Desi got in first and slid to the opposite side of the bench seat and adjusted her dress that had gotten twisted when she slid across the expensive leather.

When Marcus got in and slid next to her and the door shut behind him, she could tell that they were both aware of the presence of the other. Both of their breathing was accelerated and there was a crackle in the air. Desi was acutely aware of his scent and his heart seemed to be beating almost so loudly that she could hear it.

Marcus couldn't help himself, the need to touch Desi was too strong. He took her hand in his and caressed the back of it with his thumb. He knew that he shouldn't feel this way, but he couldn't help himself. He wanted to do things with her that he had only dreamed of before. He felt the sizzle when their skin touched. It felt almost as if he had been burned, but he knew it was just the strong physical attraction that they had. He was sure he wasn't going to be able to say no to her this weekend. It had been almost impossible when she had taken him into her mouth on his couch the night before last. He had done his best to avoid her yesterday, claiming that he was really tired and hadn't slept well the night before. This weekend, there would be nothing between them. And, as much as he knew that was wrong, he couldn't help that he wanted to find out just how good things could be between them.

Desi reached forward to press the button and the privacy glass went up. Once that was in place, she placed her upper body across Marcus's lap and kissed him deeply. He didn't seem to object.

Desi shoved her hands in his hair and pulled him more tightly to her mouth.

Marcus loved the way Desi kissed him. It was like she couldn't get enough of his touch. She sucked on his tongue, he really seemed to like that.

His hands were sliding all over her back. The dress she had chosen to wear was low cut in the back. Desi moaned; his strong hands felt so good on her bare skin. She felt the press of his erection against her hip. She shifted so that she was straddling him, she pushed the full skirt of her dress out of the way so that he was pressed against her bare skin. She hadn't worn underwear; she had planned for this to be a part of the trip. Hopefully it was the start of a long weekend of debauchery. With her knees on either side of him, she wrapped her arms around his neck and deepened the kiss. She licked at his mouth, stroking her tongue along his.

He gripped her waist and pushed her away slightly. "What are you doing?"

She ran her hands down his chest through his shirt and felt the strong muscles beneath. "I'm touching you. I love touching you."

"We shouldn't be doing this here, in the car, driving down the road. Someone might see us." he protested.

"The windows are tinted, no one can see in and with that glass up, the driver can't see or hear anything at all."

"We shouldn't be starting something like this here." he argued. "We should wait until we have time to make it really good."

"We have hours." Desi said. "We have all this nice big space, why shouldn't we enjoy some fun to waste the time.

"We shouldn't start something we can't finish for hours. I'm losing my mind just from touching and kissing you." he protested.

"So let's make sure we get it finished now." she purred.

"We can't do all of that here, in the car."

"Why not?" Although she knew exactly why he would feel that way, she wasn't going to be obvious and let on so she teased. "Haven't you ever had sex in a limo?"

"No." he replied. "Have you?"

She looked away. She wasn't sure that she wanted to give an answer, she didn't want Marcus to think of her as cheap and easy, but she needed to solidify the bond between them. She wasn't sure what was going to happen with David or how soon the assignment was over for both of them. Although she had already gotten Marcus to do a lot with her, she wanted to draw him in as much as possible. She wanted the lord of Perdition to be proud of her for completely corrupting him.

She rocked against him, rubbing her sex against the hard length of his cock. He hissed out a breath between clenched teeth. "I need you, Marcus." she said breathlessly, she leaned into his neck, inhaling his scent. The musk like smell was stronger now that he was getting aroused. It was rather intoxicating to smell him. "I need this."

He stopped trying to push her away, so she reached between them and unzipped his fly. She raised her body enough that she could free his hard shaft. "Please give me this."

He didn't relax, but he made no further attempt to stop her. When his cock fell into her hands and she started her caress, he groaned. It sounded like a combination of frustration at his own desire and need for the same thing she wanted. He was as hard as stone. She slid both of her fists up his length from root to tip. He quivered beneath her and her breath caught for a minute.

Marcus gripped her thighs, his hands sliding up her legs under the full skirt. His thumb started to try to find her slit between them. When he found his goal, he said "You're pussy is always so slick and soft. I'd love to lay you out and lick you until you beg for me." Marcus wasn't exactly sure where that statement had come from, it wasn't very poetic, but it was true. He hadn't tasted her although she had tasted him.

"I'll beg for you now if you want." She stroked him with one hand and with the other she adjusted her dress so it was less in the way of her goal to ride him.

One of his thumbs slid along the lips of her sex. "I barely touch you and you're so ready for me." he whispered.

"I can't help it." Desi said. "You're such a good lover and my body recognizes yours, it wants more and more of you."

"I don't want you to help it," he said, pressing one thumb into her. "It wouldn't be fair if I was the only one that couldn't help wanting this. I can't stop what you do to me, and I no longer want to."

"I agree completely."

"I'm breaking all of the rules with you and I can't help it." Marcus said with a low rumble.

The seriousness of his voice sent a burst of warm satisfaction through Desi and gave her more confidence to continue. Her plan was working, he was hooked. "Rules are made to be broken." she purred into his ear. She raised enough to allow him to lower his slacks more so that she could slide her went cunt down onto his shaft.

"Go slow." he ordered with a raspy gravel to his voice. He tensed when she wrapped her fingers around him to position him at the entrance to her pussy. There was a sent of lust in the air of the limo. It was heavy and humid, a seductive mix of need and pheromones that awakened every part of her body. Her skin was flushed and tingling, her breasts were heavy and her nipples tender.

This was what she had wanted form the first moment she had been given the assignment. Yes, she had wanted to make him stumble, but she had wanted some physical pleasure out of it all too. She wanted to climb up his body and take him deep inside her.

"Oh, Desi." he gasped as she had lowered herself onto him, his hands flexed restlessly on her hips.

She closed her eyes to shut out everything except the physical sensations of being so filled with him. They were in such a small space compared to anything before and it seemed like the whole compartment was filled with electricity. The world was flowing past them, but they were in their own capsule of lust and pleasure.

"You feel so tight, it's like a vise gripping me." he gasped. His words almost sounded like agony, although it was pure pleasure.

She leaned back so that the angle allowed him to go deeper. She sucked in a deep breath feeling exquisitely full.

Pressing his palm flat against her lower stomach, he reached a thumb down and rubbed her throbbing clit. He began to massage it in slow, soft circles. Everything in her core tightened and clenched, drawing him deeper. Opening her eyes she looked at him under heavy eyelids. He really was an amazing specimen of masculinity. His powerful body was succumbing to the primal need to mate.

His neck arched pressing his head firmly back against the seat back. It was like he was struggling against invisible bonds. "Oh, Desi" he ground out, his teeth almost grinding. "I'm going to come so hard."

His dark promise excited her even more than she already was. Sweat drenched her skin. She became even more soaked. She slid smoothly down the length of his cock until she had nearly sheathed him completely. An almost sob came from the back of her throat before she took him fully to the root. She couldn't help but shift side to side because her body wanted him to go deeper, but there was no way that could happen. He was already buried in her fully. Her body rippled around him, squeezing and trembling on the precipice of an orgasm that she was sure would blow her mind.

Sweat dotted his upper lip under the strain of the effort to continue to hold onto the feelings she was causing. Desi leaned forward and licked at his lip. She tasted the saltiness of his body and that just amped her up even more.

"Slow" he cautioned again. His authoritative tone sent even more lust pulsating through her entire body.

She lowered her body back down again. Taking him fully inside her. There was a luscious soreness at the fullness and the rapid pace of riding him this way.

Wild for him, she pressed her lips to his, her fingers gripping his dampened hair. They were both hot and sweaty, but she didn't care. It wasn't like the staff would dare say anything if they showed up to the house mussed from their escapades in the limo.

"It's so good." she growled. "You feel....soooo good."

Using both hands, Marcus guided her hips in the rhythm he needed her to keep. Primal instinct had taken over and he felt almost feral. He needed her to go at his pace, he needed to control this situation, he needed more. He wasn't even sure what more was, he just felt like he needed it.

She tilted at a new angle, and she could feel the crown of his cock rubbing a tender spot deep inside her. She tightened and shook, she realized she was going to come from that pressure, from his thrusts deep inside of her. "Marcus" she moaned his name as her orgasm rippled through her.

Marcus watched her fall apart. Feeling her orgasm pulse against him made him race toward his own. It was only a few moments before he felt the sensation rising up from his balls to explode out of the tip of his dick.

They sat for several minutes, Desi collapsed against his chest. After she regained her composure, she shifted her body off of him trying to be careful not to make more of a mess than there already was. She knew where the tissues were hidden in a console by the seat so she grabbed them out, took some and handed the box to Marcus.

The rest of the drive was spent just relaxing and coming down from the high they had been on.

When they pulled into the large circle drive in front of the house in the Hampton's, Marcus was dumbfounded. He had never seen a home this large on earth. Of course, the lord of Paradise had a huge home, but he wasn't going to compare the two. He didn't want to think about how much trouble he was going to be in when his assignment was done.

The driver got out and grabbed their luggage from the trunk and carried it to the doorway. It opened to an older woman standing just inside. "Miss Desire" the woman said.

"It's been ages since you've been here. I'm so glad you were able to come." She turned to Marcus and said, "I assume you are Marcus. We've prepared the two suites at the top of the left staircase for your visit."

"Thank you, Georgia." Desi said. "I'm sure everything will be perfect as always. You've run this household for years and you always do a professional job."

The woman seemed to beam at the compliment. She obviously took pride in her position here.

The driver had handed the luggage off to another man who had carried it up the stairs.

"I've prepared a light dinner for you. I wasn't sure if you had eaten yet." Georgia said. "Would you like to freshen up from you trip and I can serve it in a few minutes either on the patio or in the dining room. If anything is amiss with the rooms or the food, please don't hesitate to call for me of Peter."

"The patio will be fine." Desi said. "We'll be right back."

Desi started up the stairs, and Marcus followed her. The two rooms they had been assigned weren't bedrooms so much as a mini suite. There was a sitting room as well as a bedroom. The bathrooms were large and luxurious with whirlpool type tubs and all the luxuries one could imagine.

Marcus had to wonder if this had been a part of the reason that David hadn't seemed to want come here often. This didn't really seem like his style. It may have been one of the things that had put him off on his father-in-law too. If he felt the man rubbed his nose in their wealth, he would be more determined to be a self-made man.

Marcus didn't want to take too much time, so he didn't take a shower. He did wash up from the escapades in the car though and he changed into something more comfortable for just hanging around the house. When he was ready, he walked to the room across the hallway and knocked lightly on the door Desi had disappeared behind several minutes before. "Desi, are you in there? I'm ready to go down to dinner if you are."

She opened the door; she too had changed into something more casual. They walked down the stairs side by side. The staircase was definitely wide enough for both of them to descend without bumping into the other. She showed

Marcus to one of the many French doors that led onto a large patio in the back of the house.

There was an area set up for dining and several comfortable lounge chairs. Just beyond a short decorative fence, Marcus could see a large swimming pool. He was determined to try to fill their weekend with activities other than sex. He wasn't sure how successful he was going to be.

After they ate, Desi took him on a brief tour of the grounds. She pointed out the tennis court, the eight car garage, and the gazebo that was closer to the beach. She pointed out the small houses that she said the live in staff stayed in. She explained that Georgia and Peter were husband and wife and had managed the household staff for as long as she could remember. She told him that when she was younger, there had been nannies and a tutor that either lived on the property or lived somewhere close by.

Georgia was the cook and coordinated the maid, the other kitchen staff when they had a large gathering, and she had been in charge of overseeing anyone that cared for Desi when she was younger. Peter, it seemed was more of a butler and his only real underling was the chauffer most of the time. Again, if they were entertaining or having a lot of guests, then his duties increased.

By the end of their weekend, they had swam and played one round of tennis, which Desi aced, and Marcus stumbled through. They had gone and gotten some sun on the beach and had eaten decadent meals. They had spent far more time in bed having sex than they should have but there was a part of him that still couldn't get enough.

Chapter 12

David found himself staring at the face of one of the men from Dynacorp. The man didn't look happy. "Look, David." he said. "We've tried to be patient, but it's been months since we made you an offer. We really want to do business with you, but we can't wait forever for an answer either. If you don't want our money, there are others out there the definitely do. We're going to give you one more week to decide and then we need to move on to other investment opportunities. Besides, there are rumors that two other companies are considering looking into the same technology you want to develop. If one of those companies beats you to production, we will have wasted our money anyway."

"I understand." David said solemnly. "I'll have an answer within the deadline."

The man just gave a brief nod and walked away.

David really didn't want to take the money from them, he wasn't sure just how many of the rumors he had heard about them were true. But if the ones about them being a sort of mafia organization that didn't give any grace with loaning money worried him. But he didn't have any other options other than his father-in-law and he really didn't want to do that either.

Could he swallow his pride and take money from the man. Marcus had encouraged him to at least consider asking the man for a loan. If he could get the money without having to sacrifice any stock in his company?

He had to realize two things, swallowing his pride and asking his father-in-law was very likely the safer option, it would protect both him and Desi. He wouldn't be able to live with himself if somehow, she got hurt in all this. Secondly, he wasn't even sure that Kenneth would be willing to give him the money at all. He may still be at the mercy of Dynacorp or have to risk waiting however long it took for other investors to consider him a worthwhile investment.

When Desi woke up Sunday morning, she had a voicemail from her father asking her to call him as soon as she got the message. She called him to see what was going on.

"Desi, I'm so glad you called." he said instead of greeting her. "I have some rather disturbing news for you. I've had a private investigator following David to try to get proof of his affair. So far, we haven't gotten any, but there is another issue that has me very concerned about David. I need to know what you want me to do."

"Okay, daddy, what is it?" Desi asked. Did David have a drug abuse problem or a gambling addiction. Something had Kenneth concerned.

"He's been meeting with a group of very unsavory people." he said.

"Oh?" She wasn't sure what that meant, possibly drug dealers or something similar.

"I don't know how to ask this, Desi other than just come right out with it." The man seemed really hesitant to say more but he did continue. "Is David in some sort of financial crisis. Do you need money?"

"I know he is wanting to expand his business, something about new technology that he wants to develop. Other than that, as far as I know we are doing okay." she assured.

"The men he had met with are bad news, sweetheart. People who don't pay them back have bad things happen to them. I fear that if he has taken money from them or if he decides to do so in the future, something could happen to him or even to you. These people aren't above hurting a loved one to put pressure on the borrower." Kenneth explained.

"I had no idea, daddy." Desi said, sounding worried. "I don't know why he would be meeting with men like that."

Marcus overheard the conversation, and he was sure he knew who Kenneth was talking about. He asked Desi if he could take the phone, he had information for her father. She said "Daddy, Marcus may know what you're talking about. Here, let me put him on the phone."

Marcus took the phone. "Hello, Kenneth. May I ask what you're concerned about?"

"David is meeting with a group of men that has a bad reputation for not doing all of their business above board, if you know what I mean."

"I do." Marcus stated. "I had thought that I may have talked him out of going with Dynacorp, but if he's still meeting with them, then he's still considering them."

"Do you know why he needs money and why he hasn't come to me?" Kenneth asked.

"Well, the need for money is to develop some new technology. It's pretty cutting edge and I think he will have a gold mine on his hands, but only if he can be the first to take it to market. He still needs more research and development and as you know, that takes time and money. He is afraid that if he waits too long, someone else will beat him too it and then his discovery becomes null and void." Marcus paused and then added, "As to why he hasn't come to you, it's a matter of pride, sir. He doesn't want you to see him as a failure. He wants to be a self-made man like you are."

Kenneth paused and then said, "Well, I have to admire him for wanting to do this on his own, but I can't let him take money from those people. I fear what will happen to him or to my daughter."

"I agree." Marcus said.

"Well, don't let this spoil your weekend. I'll talk to David somehow." Kenneth said. "Oh, and on a positive note, I haven't gotten any reports of David meeting with another woman, so he may not be having an affair. I'm not sure that he isn't, but I don't have any proof of it so far."

"Yes, sir." Marcus said. "I'll pass that information along to your daughter." He disconnected the call and felt a rock in the pit of his stomach. If David wasn't having an affair, at least a portion of his justification for what he was doing with Desi was invalid. That wasn't good news for him.

Marcus knew that that was good news for Desi. It just wasn't good news for him. If David wasn't having an affair, he had allowed himself to do things he should have never considered doing with Desi because he thought turnabout was fair play.

Marcus did his best to avoid anymore contact with Desi until they left the Hampton's a few hours later. That really didn't do much to help relieve his guilt when Desi sat snuggled against him on the entire ride home. He tried to act like he was tired and just not in the mood. They really hadn't slept a lot during their weekend.

Chapter 13

Marcus had followed Desi into the office the following Wednesday. She went down the hall to check and see if David was in, but she returned saying that he wasn't. Marcus made his way to his own office. Honestly, there wasn't much for him to do. David had already heard anything he had by way of information about possible investors. There wasn't any other than Dynacorp if he wasn't willing to consider his father-in-law.

She came into his office and sat across from him. "I just don't know where he could be." she said sadly. "This really isn't like him. Or maybe it is exactly like him, if he's having an affair.

"Now, Desi." Marcus consoled. "Your father said that he didn't find any evidence that David was cheating. "

"I know but I don't really understand what he could be doing then." she argued. "Coming in here to the office seems like the best place to try to find investors, if that's what he is trying to do."

Marcus knew he shouldn't do this, but he held his arms open for Desi to come to him for a hug. "We'll figure it all out, Desi." he assured.

Desi leaned up and kissed him on the cheek, Her mouth then moved to his lips. "I don't know what I would have done all these weeks without you here to keep me sane, Marcus."

Desi was actually somewhat surprised that both of them hadn't been yanked back to their respective homes. Although she had a feeling that Marcus might be living somewhere other than Paradise soon.

She deepened the kiss and rubbed her body up against his. His cock immediately started to respond to her body. It had learned what it liked and it wasn't hesitant to show it. She stepped back two steps so that her ass was braced against his desk. She wrapped her legs around him and drew him tightly to her.

She knew it wouldn't be long before he protested, they hadn't ever done anything at the office other than that first time when she had positioned herself under his desk. She rocked against him as he became more and more aroused.

It was a few more minutes before he got his head screwed back on straight, but when he did, he told her, "We can't do this here Desi. David could walk in at any moment, or someone else could show up."

"No one ever comes here." she pouted. "It's like a dead zone."

"I know, but it is David's office and he could walk in at any time."

"Fine." she huffed. She unwrapped her legs from around him and let her feet drop to the floor.

Marcus couldn't believe how beautiful Desi was without her clothes on. He had seen her naked before, but it never failed to amaze him that anyone could be that perfect. As she walked to him, the need in his own body grew immensely. He needed to touch her; he needed to be touched by her. He reached out to her and caressed her breast. She hadn't seen him come in behind her, so she jumped a little at this touch. As soon as she realized who it was, she turned to him to give him better access to her body.

"Marcus, I'm so glad you're here. I needed to be with you tonight." she purred.

"I couldn't stay away. I needed to be inside you again. The time on my desk earlier wasn't nearly enough for me to be satisfied." he sort of growled. "I don't seem to ever be satisfied when it comes to you. I need more and more and more."

"I feel the same way." She leaned in to kiss him, she held her body far enough away that he could continue his touching her body. She was happy that the lord of Perdition had given her the ability to experience physical and sexual touch. If she didn't have that, she would still do everything in her power to seduce Marcus, but it wouldn't have been nearly as fun. This way, they both got to experience the real feeling that humans did when they got together. She had to admit she wouldn't mind being able to experience this part of being human far more often. She knew the assignment was coming to an end soon, it had to be. There was no way that the lord of Paradise was going to let this go on much longer, he wasn't sure why he had let it go on at all. He kind of thought that the first time he had kissed Desi he would have been taken back to Paradise to face a not too happy master.

He was going to tune out that thought though. He knew it wouldn't last, he was going to take advantage of whatever time he had left here on earth.

Desi was already leading him down the hall to the extra bedroom. There was something about the idea of having sex with her in the bed she shared with David that he just couldn't do. Of course, if he were honest with himself, this really wasn't any better.

As soon as they walked into the room, Desi began unbuttoning her blouse. Marcus just stood and watched for a long while, until Desi asked him if he was going to join her. He started undressing as well. As soon as he had his shirt off, Desi was right there in front of him helping him remove his pants. She unzipped them and let them fall to his feet. She got down to her knees and took him in her mouth. He had never felt anything so good in his life except for being inside her pussy. Her mouth was amazing. The way she swirled her tongue around the shaft when she had him mostly in her mouth. The way she pulled away to just lick the tip. Then going back down on him to let him feel the back of her throat. It was then that he felt her swallow and he almost lost it. If this was his first time, he probably would have, but he had learned over the time that he had been with her that he could control himself better than he would have thought. He knew that a part of that was the end goal of being buried in her slick wet pussy. This was just the prelude to the icing on the cake as he had heard humans say.

He could only take so much of it before he needed to make her stop and move on to something else. If he didn't, she wouldn't get any pleasure from him. He loved that she wanted to be the one to give him pleasure, but he wanted to reciprocate too.

He put a hand on each side of her face and gently pushed her away. "No, Desi, please I need to be able to taste you too." he panted.

Desi looked up at him with a pout, however she did let him pull her away from his cock. He lifted her onto the bed and spread her legs open for him. His cock was begging him to just plunge inside her already, but he told it to shut up. He laid his body on the bottom half of the bed and put his face down to her sweet smell. He could stay here and just inhale her scent for hours. Except, that wouldn't get either one of them where they wanted to go. He did indulge himself for a few more moments.

He inhaled one more deep breath before he lowered his head and began to lick at her delicious juices. She tasted amazing. He had nothing to compare it to, he obviously hadn't done anything remotely like this before Desi, but it tasted sweeter than any treat he had ever experienced.

He licked at her slit, making sure to pay special attention to the small hard nub. Every time he did that, she squirmed beneath him as if it were driving her crazy. "Marcus, please."

"Please, what?" he asked trying to seem totally clueless. He knew exactly what she wanted. He had gone beyond watching the Hallmark channel to things that were far more sexy. He was smart enough to know that porn wasn't really accurate, he had found other channels that were sort of between porn and the sweet clean love stories the greeting card company owned. From some channels, he had learned how to satisfy both Desi and himself physically, but he had learned from the Hallmark channel that he was pretty sure he was starting to fall for Desi. It wasn't just a physical attraction for him.

He hadn't declared anything yet. He thought maybe Desi was feeling the same way, but he wasn't sure and he didn't want to make himself out to be the fool in all of this. She was still a married woman after all. She hadn't said anything about leaving David or ending things with him, so Marcus wasn't sure exactly where he stood.

Desi was squirming so much it was difficult to continue. Not only that, he didn't think his cock could take much more before it exploded all over the bed rather than inside of her. He raised himself up onto his knees and positioned himself at the entrance of her hole. He put the tip in slowly, but once that was lined up, he plowed forward with full force, burying himself completely in her warmth. He paused for just a minute while his eyes rolled to the back of his head with how good this felt. It was beyond amazing. He didn't have the words. Desi shifted a little beneath him, most likely trying to urge him on to get moving. She didn't have to request that twice.

He began with slower strokes, just to completely feel the friction and the tightness of her around him, that only lasted a few strokes before he had to speed up the pace. The increase in friction caused a feeling that he couldn't even come up with the words to describe. Amazing, Insane, Incredible, wonderful, awesome, marvelous, sublime, and heavenly came to mind. He couldn't hold out any longer.

"Come with me, Desi." he commanded. He pounded into her a few more times and just before he couldn't hold out any longer and his release was imminent, he felt her cunt squeezing tightly around him.

David sat across the table from his father-in-law. "I swear to you Kenneth, I'm not cheating on Desi. I've been completely immersed in trying to find investors for my project and getting as far with the prototype as I can without those investors. I didn't realize what I was doing to Desi.

I will back off on the areas that I can and spend more time making sure that she knows that I still love her beyond reason."

"If you needed money, why didn't you come to me? I'd be happy to invest in your company, after all, it's investing in my daughter's future as well" Kenneth said.

"I didn't want to get you involved. I guess my pride got in my way. I didn't want you to think that I couldn't provide a good life for your daughter." David said humbly.

"Nonsense." Kenneth scoffed. "Everyone needs help at times to step into their potential. I wouldn't be the success I am today if I hadn't been born into a life of wealth and privilege."

David just nodded his head in understanding.

"Tell me what you need David. I'll make it a loan with no interest compounded on it. You don't even have to tell anyone where you got the money. I won't hold this over your head. I honestly believe that you can do this thing. I don't understand everything about your discoveries. I'm not a tech guy, I've heard rumors of good things. In fact, I'd love to be a shareholder in your company, I think the profit potential is huge. I won't push for that if you just want the money with no strings attached other than a very lenient repayment plan."

"I have no problem with giving you a portion of stock, as long as I always retain the controlling interest." David said. "I was being selfish and wasn't thinking about how this is all effecting Desi. I should have done better and I promise that I will do so in the future."

Kenneth reached out his hand and said, "Since technology moves faster than I do, we can work out the specific details another time. Just tell me how much you need to get this thing done."

David listed an amount that most individuals would flinch at, finance companies wouldn't have had a problem, but most individuals didn't have that kind of money. Kenneth on the other hand reached into his pocket and pulled out his phone. He sent a text to someone and then said, "Let's have a drink to celebrate your up and coming project."

While they were enjoying a scotch on the rocks, David felt his phone vibrate. He pulled it out to find a notification from his bank letting him know that the amount he had requested from Kenneth had been deposited into his account with a fifty thousand dollar bonus. He looked at the man dumbfounded at how the man had accomplished that.

"Don't worry about it, just use the bonus to do something nice with my daughter. A short getaway perhaps to reassure her that you are still totally committed to her." Kenneth said with a smile.

They finished their scotch; they walked out together. As David walked toward his car, a single gunshot rang out from somewhere in the distance.

Chapter 14

The lord of Paradise didn't have to turn around to know that his biggest adversary was standing right behind him.

"What do you think of your star pupil now?" he sneered. "Didn't quite live up to what you had hoped, now did he?"

"No, but then again, I didn't plan on your substituting Esmerelda for the real Desi either." the lord of Paradise said. "I firmly believe that if it had been the real Desi, he would have done exactly as I had hoped."

"Oh, come now." the lord of Perdition said. "You didn't expect me to just sit back and not try to sabotage things did you?"

"I had hoped that it would be at least a fair fight."

"Where is the fun in that?" the lord of Perdition asked. "It's not really much of a challenge to let him go up against a woman who is totally devoted to her husband."

"What did you do with the real Desire?

"She's safe." the dark lord said. "Don't worry. We didn't harm her, we just let her fall asleep, for a long time. She'll never know the difference. Well, other than waking up to her husband being dead."

"You're despicable, do you know that?"

"Well, it's kind of my nature, you know." he gave a maniacal chuckle. "It's what I do."

The lord of Paradise just shook his head.

"Admit it, he's mine now, isn't he?" he gloated. "You can't possibly be willing to forgive him for such a horrific failure on his assignment, can you? Not to mention how much he debased himself."

"Yes, he's yours." the lord of Paradise finally admitted. "You're right, I can't let this slide."

"Wonderful." And then the lord of Perdition was gone.

Marcus closed his eyes and leaned in to taste Desi's lips just one more time before he had to leave to go and find David. He knew that he shouldn't have been doing any of this, but for some reason, he just couldn't seem to help himself.

Suddenly, he didn't feel her in his arms anymore and there was a heavy weight on his back. It felt almost like his wings when he was in Paradise. He realized all of this in a millisecond and opened his eyes. He was standing in front of the Lord of Paradise and he did not look at all happy.

He knew this was not going to go well, but maybe if he explained to the boss that he was just getting ready to go and meet David and keep him from the meeting with the triad because Desi had secured the funding from her father. He needed to get back to earth to be able to do that. His boss could scold him later about the inappropriate relationship with Desi. "Hey boss, I know we have a lot of things to talk about, however I really need to get back to earth. David is just getting ready to go and meet with the bad guys and accept their offer of money. I need to stop him and tell him that he already has the funding."

The god just nodded skeptically for a minute. "It would be great if you could go back and do just that. The problem is that David died."

Marcus was shocked speechless for a second. "Wait, what do you mean, dead? He was going to tell them he was taking the money. Why would they kill him? I was going to talk him out of that of course, and then help him deal with them being angry over the loss of the contract."

"Except, you didn't count on Kenneth being the type that wants everyone to know how magnanimous he is and he called a press conference to announce his merger with his son-in-law's company. As soon as the triad heard that, they put out a mark on David's head and it didn't take long for that to be dealt with."

"Send me back down there, you can turn the time back enough so that I can get to him and protect him." Marcus pleaded.

"Unfortunately, that isn't how this works, Marcus. You were given an assignment and not only did you fail to complete it, but your debauchery with his wife is also inexcusable. No, Marcus, this isn't something you can go back and correct. You're banished from Paradise, forever."

Marcus's wings felt hot he turned to look at them, and they were changing from the normal white to a deep gray and black. "Please, forgive me. I'll fix it, if you'll only give me a chance."

"No, Marcus, I'm sending you to Perdition for your utter failure on your assignment and your horrible behavior with a man's wife. Don't ever try to seek forgiveness, it won't come."

Everything went dark and Marcus knew that he was standing at the edge of Perdition, a gate opened and a voice said "Welcome Marcus, I've been waiting for you."

Marcus wasn't sure what to say. There was nothing to say really, he had made a horrible mess of things and he had been justly punished for it. What he hadn't expected when the gate opened further was to see Desire, the woman that he had fallen for not only physically and emotionally, but also spiritually.

"Desi, what are you doing here?" he asked.

"Oh, that's not Desire, not the real one anyway. That's the decoy that I sent to earth to take you down. I knew you were weak and would fall for her easily." the lord of Perdition chuckled.

"What happened to the real Desire?"

"Oh, she's been safely asleep in a hospital bed for the last several weeks, although, she's awake now, and she's sadly grieving her husband's death."

And Marcus knew that was all on him. Even if it had been a decoy that he had fallen in love with, he had caused her husband's death. Oh, he hadn't pulled the trigger, but he might as well have, he had neglected to keep the man safe and, in the end, his would be partners hadn't liked the fact that he had reneged on their deal and they had taught him a lesson.

The ramifications of what he had done hit him so hard, he could barely stand. He would figure out a way to go back and make this right. He didn't know how, and he knew he couldn't bring the man back, but maybe, he could find a way to help Desire find her way through this. He would just have to bide his time and do his best to earn the respect of his new 'boss'. Maybe then he could get an assignment back on earth.

Made in the USA
Monee, IL
23 March 2025